CW01501801

Praise for Michelle Paver's Previous Supernatural Novels

'Paver is the mistress of suspense'
THE TIMES

'Terror on a grander scale'
THE GUARDIAN

'A tale of terror and beauty and wonder'
THE FINANCIAL TIMES

'A tense and strangely beautiful narrative'
METRO

'Spellbindingly creepy'
THE SUNDAY EXPRESS

'An elegantly told tale with a vivid sense of place –
and it's deeply scary'
THE SYDNEY HERALD

'Holds you in a vice-like grip'
SCI-FI NOW

'Chilling in every sense'
THE MAIL ON SUNDAY

Michelle Paver was born in central Africa and came to England as a child. After gaining a degree in Biochemistry from Oxford University, she worked as a solicitor before giving up the law to write full-time. Her books include the internationally bestselling Wolf Brother series for younger readers, and the acclaimed supernatural novels *Dark Matter*, *Thin Air*, and *Wakenhyrst*.

www.michellepaver.com

RAINFOREST

MICHELLE PAVER

ORION

First published in Great Britain in 2025 by Orion Fiction,
an imprint of The Orion Publishing Group Ltd.,
Carmelite House, 50 Victoria Embankment
London EC4Y 0DZ

The authorised representative in the EEA is Hachette Ireland,
8 Castlecourt Centre, Castleknock Road, Castleknock, Dublin 15,
D15 XTP3, Republic of Ireland (email: info@hbgi.ie)

An Hachette UK Company

1 3 5 7 9 10 8 6 4 2

A CIP catalogue record for this book is
available from the British Library.

ISBN (Hardback) 9781398723207
ISBN (Export Trade Paperback) 9781398723214
ISBN (eBook) 9781398723238
ISBN (Audio) 9781398723245

Typeset by Input Data Services Ltd, Bridgwater, Somerset

Printed in Great Britain by Clays Ltd, Elcograf, S.p.A.

www.orionbooks.co.uk

Also by Michelle Paver

Supernatural Novels
Dark Matter
Thin Air
Wakenhyrst

For Younger Readers

The Wolf Brother Novels (*the first six comprising*
Chronicles of Ancient Darkness)
Wolf Brother
Spirit Walker
Soul Eater
Outcast
Oath Breaker
Ghost Hunter
Viper's Daughter
Skin Taker
Wolfbane

Gods and Warriors
The Outsiders
The Burning Shadow
The Eye of the Falcon
The Crocodile Tomb
Warrior Bronze

One

Room 13, Hotel Santo Domingo, Mexico City

I'm writing this sitting on the bed with the talisman in my free hand. The ceiling fan's wobbling and the overhead light is flickering. The shadows slicing the walls are making me dizzy.

I didn't sleep on the flight from Heathrow or from Jamaica and I won't sleep tonight. A cicada is rasping, he's quite extraordinarily loud. I've searched the whole room but I can't find the little bugger. He could be anywhere, cicadas are brilliant ventriloquists.

I know what you'd say about getting to sleep, Dr Walker, but I can't take one of your pills. Early flight tomorrow to some little town in the mountains, then a charter plane to the jungle and a boat up a river. I don't know its name and I don't want to. I just need to get away.

I never told you about the talisman, did I? It's the size of my thumb, neatly shrouded in my handkerchief. After I'd had the first coffee with her we were saying goodbye under our birch tree when her hair snagged on a twig and she pulled it free. When she'd gone I went back and retrieved several long black strands and snapped off the twig and wound them round. I've had the talisman ever since. I keep it zipped in the breast pocket of my safari shirt, against my heart. I don't care if that's sentimental. I will keep it always.

Just now I wrote that I have to get away, but I know I can't do that, not ever, because she's dead. I can never get away from that.

You see how it always comes back to her, Dr Walker? That's why I can't sleep. That's why I've done what you suggested and started this journal. And maybe you're right, maybe writing will stop the thoughts going round and round like angry wasps.

Although I'm not going to write about Penelope. Why should I? No point re-hashing the past. This is about the future. A clean break.

I found that cicada. He was hiding behind the picture of the Virgin Mary above the bed. He's been driving me mad and when I found him, I wanted to squash him. Me, the insect lover! I was shocked.

Of course I thought better of it. He is so beautiful. Some kind of *Zammara*, I think. His transparent wings are deceptively delicate, folded over a powerful body that's boldly marked in turquoise and black. How can I blame him for disturbing me when all he's doing is trying to attract a mate?

Some hope in here, poor sod. I've stowed him in my pocket, I'm going to take him outside and find him a home. I spotted some oleanders on the corner of the street. Who knows, maybe he'll even find a female.

One thing's for certain. I can't stay in this room any longer. It's supposed to be winter in Mexico but it's hot as hell and the walls feel as if they're closing in. I can't stand this bloody flickering.

Well that was a mistake. The Day of the Dead was *last* week, for Christ's sake, I booked my flights specifically to avoid it – but you'd never guess, the shops and street stalls bristling with sugar skulls and cheery plastic skeletons in all the colours of the rainbow. It was horrible. Not to mention the traffic fumes and the blaring horns, the cacophony of Spanish – which I don't speak.

I left my cicada in an oleander bush. Better luck out here, my friend. I didn't want to leave him, he'd been company. The crowds on the street were making me uneasy, so I sought refuge in the nearest museum.

And where did I end up? Staring into a glass case at a big pear-shaped bundle of earth-coloured cloth two thousand years old, containing the mummified remains of a human being. A cutaway diagram revealed the thing inside, crouching in a basket, its skeletal knees drawn up to its chest, its shrunken face half-hidden by bony fingers. A caption in broken English said the body was wrapped in many layers of '*elaporated cloths*'. Like a giant sweet.

Why of all things did I have to stumble across a corpse? Why not some harmless collection of pots? Wretched object wasn't even Mexican, the sign said it was borrowed from Peru. That makes me feel as if I've been singled out. Why can't death leave me alone?

I should have walked away, but I couldn't stop staring. The thing was lopsided, its head cocked as if slyly peering

3

up at me. Its earthy outer wrapping was patterned with little faded motifs in green and yellow, they looked like hummingbirds and bees. The night we met she was wearing a floaty frock embroidered with butterflies and tiny coin-sized mirrors. I said it was nice, and she said it was from India and she was 'into ethnic stuff'. I hadn't a clue what she meant, not being familiar with how her generation speaks. That made her laugh. Later she told me she'd only been trying out a 'look' and wasn't particularly 'into' ethnic stuff, she'd said it as a joke.

That was the whole problem, I never could tell when she was teasing. That's why it all went wrong.

A party of tourists drifted past, their voices soughing and receding like waves. I felt sweat trickling down my spine, caught a whiff of my unwashed flesh. Not bees, I thought muzzily. Hornets. Although are hornets indigenous to Mexico? I'll have to look that up.

A Mexican matron waddled up and crossed herself when she saw the carcase. All at once I wanted to strangle her, an uprush of pure heart-thumping rage. And it wasn't only her I was angry with, it was everyone. Those ancient Peruvians with their bundled corpse, what did they *imagine* they were achieving? And Mexicans with their Day of the Dead? Do you really think it's that easy? Chuck a few sugary treats on the grave and she'll come back?

I've had these spurts of rage since my breakdown, but knowing they're only a symptom doesn't make them easier to deal with. I lost my temper with Wanda, poor little cow, and her unthinking belief that the dead live on. You remember Wanda, Dr Walker, Jeremy's wife? He's my best friend (well, my only friend), they came to visit me in hospital? I've known them since we were at Cambridge and I like her, I do, even if she is a bit of a hippie, and strident about Women's Lib. But all that drivel about death being merely 'passing over', 'one door closing, another opening'. That's such rubbish. It's how the living fool themselves into believing they're still connected to the dead – when the truth is, there's nothing to be connected *to*.

'Rest in peace'? That makes me so *angry*. How can Penelope be at peace when she no longer exists? She isn't 'resting'. *She – is – not*. That's what I can't bear.

Wanda would probably say that it wasn't by chance that I ended up in front of that carcase in the museum, she'd tell me it was Fate. Well fuck that, Wanda. What's Fate – what's faith – but belief without evidence? If you want to believe in a soul which lives on after death, fine, go ahead. Just so long as you admit that it's on a par with believing there's a leprechaun in my sock drawer. Both ideas are founded on nothing.

The museum was emptying. As I crossed the echoing hall I felt unreal, cut off from everyone. I watched myself politely making way for an old lady and her granddaughter, while inside I felt the howl gathering force, pushing up into my throat like a fist. Pull yourself together, Simon, you can't break down here. No crouching on the floor with your head in your hands, like those huddled remains.

Out in the street, self-preservation kicked in. I didn't fancy being mugged and left for dead in an alleyway, so I squared my shoulders and feigned assurance, in case any thieves were watching.

My cicada was still rasping away in his bush. I felt sorry

for him; he belongs in the rainforest, high in the canopy. And he put me in mind of where I'm going.

On the flight from Jamaica I looked at my field guides, and for the first time since it happened, I felt a twinge of excitement. So many species of mantid – such riches waiting to be discovered. Thinking of that now, I realise that the jungle isn't merely an escape, I do actually want to be there. I need that dense green tangled dimness; the flutter and hum of insect lives.

And I find the fact that I'm still capable of longing quite encouraging. Perhaps you're right, Dr Walker, perhaps I am getting better. And surely it's a hopeful sign that I care about not being mugged?

It seems that I really do want to reach the rainforest alive.

All that rage in the museum. That contempt for the sugar skulls and the ancient people with their pathetic wrapped remains. And yet here am I with my talisman: a dead woman's hair wrapped round a twig. Why do I keep it, if not from a primitive belief that this tiny part of her contains her spirit?

Or at least her essence – which in a way it does, her DNA. The primitive aspect lies in my belief, unconscious but undoubtedly there, that by touching this part of her, as I am doing now – all right, not touching, clutching – that by clutching these strands of her hair, I am touching her. There's the self-deception. The pitiable attempt to deny death.

I *know* all this. I know that this twig is merely an assemblage of lignin, these strands of hair are simply twisted chains of keratin. It's not *her*. And yet this talisman feels charged. Radioactive.

So let's be honest, shall we? Let's not deceive ourselves. It wasn't contempt that I felt for those people in the museum, it was envy. If only I was like them. If only I too could believe that I can contact the dead. That I could see her, touch her one last time.

If only, if only, if only. That's why I can't sleep. That's why I need the jungle. If anything can save me, it's my mantids. We're in this together, my beauties. It's you and me against the world.

Two

I'm on the plane to San Cristóbal and the woman beside me has been reading over my shoulder. Podgy, forty-ish, plain. Beige slacks, flowery blouse, probably bought new for the trip; hardly any make-up, fingernails painted a careful pink. She's smoking too much, clearly eager to chat. Well, she was; and if she's reading this now, too bad, it serves you right for snooping.

Earlier she told me she hated flying and would I mind if we talked? I said okay, and she asked how long I'd be staying in San Cristóbal. Only a night, I said, someone's meeting me, tomorrow we're off to the jungle.

Her eyes widened in admiration. 'Sounds intrepid.'

'Not really. I gather it's an established camp, been going for years, some sort of dig. Although I won't be—'

'Ooh, you're an archaeologist! So's my boss! Maybe you met him at the conference in Chiapas?'

'I'm not an archaeologist.'

'Oh. So why go to the jungle?'

Nettled, I pointed out of the window at the clouds. 'There's a forest down there. I'm an entomologist. I study insects.'

She gave a theatrical little shudder. People often do, especially women. You'd think I'd be used to it by now, but I still find it annoying. A few days ago I was in Stanford's buying maps and I picked up a *'Traveller's Guide to Mexican Wildlife'*. It had lavish sections on Birds, Mammals, Reptiles, Amphibians and Fish – but *nothing* on insects. It was all I could do not to tear the bloody thing apart. How can they ignore the most successful phylum on the planet? Sometimes I think that's what drew me to insects in the first place: because they're unloved.

Anyway, a few minutes ago I got my neighbour to shut up by telling her about my breakdown. It worked a treat, she flashed me a meaningless smile and shrank back in her seat. Then an air hostess came with a tray and we both took plastic cups of pink pop and exchanged polite nods, mutely acknowledging that we won't speak again till we've landed and are saying goodbye.

She's pretending to be absorbed in her book. It's open at a double-page picture done in that brutal Central American style, maybe Aztec or Inca? Colours are nice and bright, but it's far too complicated, I can't make out what it's meant to be. I find it unsettling. I hope there's nothing like it on the dig. Although if there is it won't matter, I'll be off in the jungle with my mantids. Yes. I must hold onto that.

Earlier when we were taking off, my neighbour glanced at my hands, I think she was checking for a wedding ring. I felt like saying, Nope, I'm not married or divorced, nor am I interested in a one-night stand. I wonder what she'd say if I told her I'm forty-two and never had a proper girlfriend until Penelope?

I never told you that, did I, Dr Walker? Before Penelope I'd had precious little to do with females. Growing up, there was Mother and my sister Marjorie, who didn't count. Let's see, at six I was infatuated with Snow White, then at eight it was Olivia de Havilland in *Robin Hood*. My older brother Edwin and I went to a boys' grammar; so the only real girls I encountered were Marjorie's friends – whom I loathed, because of their affected terror of my stick insects.

When adolescence struck, I moved on to more actresses: Jean Simmons, Anna Neagle, and the girl in the Playtex advert. No real female showed an interest in me, except to mock. I was such an easy target: too tall, too thin, too tongue-tied to fight back.

Of course I was aware of the Swinging Sixties, how could I not be, with my colleagues at the Institute busily coupling and uncoupling? But somehow it never applied to me. I've always felt like a separate species. People think insects don't have hearts, but they do, they're just different from ours. That's how I felt, different. And I was fine with it, I didn't *want* to join in. I was happy with my mantids.

I'm not trying to excuse myself, there is no excuse for what I did. All I'm saying is that if I'd known more about women when I met Penelope, it might not have happened.

Just now I was gazing out of the window when the clouds parted and suddenly there was the rainforest – a vast, shimmering green wilderness. I felt a stinging behind my eyes. I realised I'd stopped breathing.

Far below me lay a shining river like a fat copper snake. I made out the tiny bronze speck of a settlement, and a narrow red slash, maybe left by loggers or coffee-planters.

Then the ravages of people were left behind like a bad dream and I saw nothing but trees.

I suppose it's because I grew up near a forest that they've always been my refuge. I feel better simply gazing down at that endless green expanse.

It's occurred to me that the worst has already happened. There can be no pain more intense than what I've experienced. No deeper disgrace, no fiercer remorse. It's all behind me.

My neighbour is still chain-smoking, still buried in her book, poring over that wall painting or whatever it's supposed to be. It's like a puzzle, but I'm beginning to make it out. It's some sort of nobleman or maybe a priest, standing in profile. He has an imposing Roman nose and a jutting lower jaw, but the back of his skull is weirdly flattened, as if someone's bashed it in. He's wearing a spotted cloak, an elaborate headdress with feathers, and odd high-sided sandals. In one fist he's grasping a leaf-shaped blade and in the other he's

What the hell? Yup, he's clutching his erect penis. It's spouting four little scarlet snakes, complete with tiny forked tongues. Are they meant to be blood? Oh God is that what he's just done with the knife?

I felt nauseous but I didn't throw up and now I'm okay. Had to re-evaluate my neighbour, though. Shortly after take-off she patted her book and told me she was 'into' pre-Columbian art, 'Though obviously not as a collector, not at those prices.' But why would anyone want to collect *that*? A man attacking his own penis with a knife?

The things people do. I don't care if it was thousands of years ago, it makes me want to vomit.

I need the jungle as never before. Please, please, I can't bear it any more. I need to be in the rainforest, alone among trees. Far away from people. Yes. Nothing human.

Things will be better down there.

Three

San Cristóbal, Later

I've seen Penelope.

She was in the market-place, standing silent and still in the crowd, Indians and *mestizos* milling around her like a river breaking round a stone. She was glaring at me the way she did that day outside the mansion block. Accusing. Then someone bumped against me and when I looked again she wasn't there. It was all I could do to stumble back to the guest house.

I'm holed up in my room. It's chilly and smells of petrol. Dogs and chickens outside, motorbikes puttering. Sounds keep flaring and receding. My eyes are scratchy with fatigue.

Earlier it rained, a real tropical downpour that lasted an hour. Across the road three black vultures are hunched in a tree, their wings half-spread to dry, like giant bats. Beneath them the ground is littered with rotting fruits the size of plums, but a dark velvety brown. Whatever they are they must be fermenting, because I've just seen a huge butterfly, a king swallowtail I think, rise drunkenly and fly away.

San Cristóbal is all narrow streets and little plazas, squat Spanish houses with red-tiled roofs and iron-barred windows. It's in the mountains, seven thousand feet up, and I've never had altitude sickness before, but I do now – hence Penelope. Altitude sickness is well known to cause hallucinations. That's what she was.

Altitude sickness also causes headaches, hence the steel band crushing my skull. And I've burst a blood vessel in my left eye, it's turned the white an alarming scarlet. When I collected my key from the desk, the woman gave me a startled look, and out of the corner of my eye I saw her cross herself.

I won't go down to supper, I shall stay in here until tomorrow, when I meet the fellows from the dig. Penelope was an artefact of altitude and fatigue. I know that. But I won't risk another encounter.

Besides, I find those Indians unsettling. Their cast of features reminds me of that picture on the plane. According to my guidebook, many of the tribes around here are direct descendants of the ancient Maya. That's surprising, I thought they'd died out centuries ago. The book says the modern ones are mostly Catholics due to the missionaries, but they also revere their local shamans, I think that's a kind of witch doctor. Apparently the Indians believe that such men can contact the spirits.

I wish I hadn't read that. I hope there aren't any Indians on the dig.

Four

Piedras Quemadas Camp, on a tributary of Rio Lacantún, s/e Chiapas

Made it to the jungle! I can't quite believe it.

Night has fallen with brutal suddenness and moths are circling the lightbulb hanging from the rafter; they keep cutting across my light. I'm breathing in swampy heat and a rank sweetness of rotting vegetation, in my ears the rhythmic rasp of billions of insects. I'm almost happy.

I'm writing this in my 'lab'. It's really only a hut at the edge of camp, and like all the others it's merely a palm-thatched roof on posts. No walls, an earth floor strewn with palm fronds. Everything open to the night.

My 'desk' is a rough board on trestles, and ten feet from where I sit, I can see a shadowy stand of heliconia. Beyond that, the black wall of the jungle.

I like the heliconia. I like its big rubber-plant leaves and its huge lobster-claw 'flowers' (they're actually bracts). It's a treasure-trove of arthropods, and before the light died I couldn't resist a swift inspection. Found three glasswings of spectral beauty, an iridescent jewel beetle and more ants and spiders than I could count. A dead leaf turned out to be a bush cricket; a nine-inch stick insect took to the air with a flash of yellow wings. *Such* riches! No mantids as yet, but that would be greedy on my first night.

I've enjoyed unpacking my gear. Plastic sheets, blowers, aspirators, pyrethrin for fogging; specimen bottles, relaxation chambers, nets, ethyl acetate, killing jars. Setting everything in order has been oddly reassuring, I suppose because my equipment is the one aspect of my work I can control.

Apart from two trestle tables, I have two canvas chairs and four tea chests fitted with padlocks, that's to keep out the spider monkeys, I've been warned about them. My gear is now securely locked up, and when I finish writing I shall lock up this journal too, safe from prying eyes. Birkenshaw strikes me as the nosey type.

There's a wasp's nest on the roof post behind me, a tiny one made of mud by a docile little potter wasp. I can't help remembering the wasps' nest I found in the shed when I was seven. I was hiding from Edwin when a wasp landed on my forearm. I kept still to avoid being stung, and the creature probed my skin with tiny delicate forelimbs. It was the first time I'd ever truly *seen* an insect – I mean, been aware of its separate existence. I watched it fly back to the nest. I saw how its fellows greeted it.

Later that day, I looked up wasps in the encyclopaedia. I was captivated. Each wasp knows its function and performs it: no doubts, no mistakes, no misunderstandings. The beautiful logic of insect lives. A million miles from the messy irrationality of human beings.

In the weeks that followed, I returned to the shed again and again. I watched those wasps for hours. I brought them offerings of windfalls. I wanted to know everything about them. I wanted to *be* one, flying through the forest on swift sure wings. I can't think of them now without sadness and guilt.

But that's in the past. I'm here now, I've reached sanctuary. And it's not just an escape, it's an opportunity. If I can do worthwhile work, something fit for publication, I'm pretty sure I can get tenure.

A fresh start. That's the ticket.

It seems like a week since we left San Cristóbal. I can't believe it was only this morning.

Ridley and Birkenshaw picked me up after breakfast. Birkenshaw's a Billy Bunter type and seems okay, but I didn't take to Ridley. He treated me like an amateur and lost no time in establishing his own credentials. 'Anthropologist, explorer, escapee from the rat race,' he said with a knowing grin. Myself, I'd call him an ageing hippie.

He's a chain-smoker with a drinker's blotchy features, and defiantly filthy: grimy canvas hat, safari shirt and trousers, muddy combat boots. A grizzled beard and a *ponytail*, for heaven's sake, the man's fifty if he's a day! Added to which, he kept us waiting at the guesthouse, then didn't apologise when he finally turned up, just said he had 'business' at the local museum.

Birkenshaw hailed him with a clap on the back. 'This is the man you need to talk to when it comes to Indians,' he told me – as if I'd asked. 'Our Ridley keeps them in line on the dig. Labour relations, that sort of thing.' He sniggered as if at some private joke.

Ridley shot him a glance. 'They're amazing people,' he told me coolly. 'Closest thing to an ancient Maya you'll ever meet. I speak the dialect. Come to me when you need to talk to them.'

'I hardly think that's likely,' I said.

That seemed to annoy him, and he took it upon himself to check over my gear. Bloody cheek. And of course he discovered that I was missing all sorts of essentials – which he then supplied with irritating relish. Disposable lighters, antibiotic pills, snake-bite serum, finger-sized aluminium cylinders of powdered sulphur for disinfecting wounds, a whistle for distress calls ('Camp Regs, the Prof insists you carry it at all times'). Plus a set of fish-hooks and fishing lines.

'But I've never fished in my life,' I protested.

'Let's hope you never have to start,' he said. 'This lot's in case you get lost.'

'And I suppose this is too?' I remarked, drawing a foot-long steel machete from its leather sheath.

'Nope, you'll carry that with you always.'

I nodded gravely. 'In case a jaguar leaps out at me on my way to the latrine.'

He threw me a look. 'Jungle's no joke, Dr Corbett. People go missing all the time. Back-packers, *chicleros* – they collect gum–'

'I know,' I said.

He looked at me. 'Even Indians go missing. Sometimes the body turns up. Mostly it doesn't.'

'I'm not new to the tropics,' I retorted. 'I've done field-work in the West Indies.'

He snorted. 'The West Indies! Where we're going, it's the real thing.'

Oh, give me strength.

A few hours later we nearly had a row. After a bumpy flight the Cessna had dropped us at the airstrip; that's what sparked the row. I'd been expecting a narrow stretch of red earth amid lush, steaming green jungle – but instead we'd landed in a treeless devastation of bleeding stumps. It was horrible. No life except for swarms of mosquitoes.

'Who did this?' I demanded as we stood in the glaring sun, waiting for the dugout to come and pick us up.

'Loggers of course,' said Ridley, lighting one of his end-less cigarettes. 'Big business round here. They're working their way slowly upstream, clearing as they go.'

It was the way he said it, so casually. '*Clearing?*' I ex-ploded. 'A forest doesn't need '*clearing*', it's not a disease! What you mean is killed.'

He was taken aback. 'For Christ's sake, they're only trees.'

I stared at him. '*Only* trees? And you say you know the jungle? My God, man, this is the wholesale destruction of a world!'

'Steady on, old fellow,' said Birkenshaw. 'Let's not get carried away. Kiss and make up, all right?'

I was breathing hard, Ridley stiff-faced, intent on his cigarette. I muttered an apology, told him I hadn't slept in days. He said no problem and we shook hands. Although afterwards I caught him exchanging an eye-roll with Birkenshaw. I shall have to watch myself. Can't go flying off the handle like that. A fresh start, remember?

I suspect that's what Ridley and Birkenshaw were after too, when they came out here. I gather from Ridley that Birkenshaw once taught at a rather good university, but left under a cloud; he didn't say why. As for Ridley, I have my suspicions. Although I may be wrong.

Things improved once the dugout puttered into sight. We loaded our gear and soon the loggers' devastation was slipping behind, and the jungle closing in.

It started to rain, a full-blooded tropical downpour. I huddled under the canvas roof rigged up at the rear of the boat, Birkenshaw beside me, wiping his glasses. 'And they call this the dry season!' he laughed, raising his voice above the din. I loved it. It felt cleansing and real.

It lasted three hours, then abruptly stopped. Clouds of mosquitoes swarmed. I took off my waterproof and sprayed on the DEET.

A white mist rose from the forest, and I breathed a fug of diesel and riverine decay. The water was a muddy, opaque green. No banks. We glided past walls of tangled vegetation so dense they were almost black.

In all the time we'd been on the river I hadn't seen any animals, not even a bird. At one point the water in the midstream mounded over something swimming level with us and I raised my binoculars; but whatever it was sank out of sight. Later we were passing through a dim green tunnel when the branches overhead suddenly thrashed, stirred by some unseen creature.

Ridley gave me his knowing grin. 'Newbies always wonder why they can't spot the wildlife.'

'Well I don't,' I said. 'I know it'll take me a few days to get my eye in.'

'Take longer than that.' His grin vanished, and he jerked his head at the handsome Indian boy at the tiller. 'Name's J.C. He'll be your guide if you leave camp. You're lucky to have him. What he doesn't know about the jungle isn't worth knowing.'

I didn't reply. What did he mean, 'if'? Of course I'll be leaving camp. Does he expect the mantids to come to me?

Just then we passed an enormous tree that towered above the canopy. Its outstretched arms were festooned with ferns and vines, its huge buttressed roots jutted like spurs. A kapok tree: tallest species in the jungle. Out here the name for it is 'ceiba', pronounced *seeba*, with a hiss. Like a snake. I've studied similar giants in Jamaica, but this one was different, its spurs were covered in spikes. As we slid past I felt a tingle of anticipation. What mantids might I discover on such a tree?

Thinking about it now gives me another twinge of excitement. Those trees are where I'll find my mantids, I'm sure of it. I can't wait to get into the jungle. Fog a ceiba, see what comes down.

A hawk moth has just flickered through the lab. They feed on night-blooming orchids, and can see colours in the dark. I wonder what that's like.

Spending even this brief time with insects has replenished me, I feel like a glass being slowly filled with clear water. 'Insect' means 'cut body' in Greek, but that doesn't begin to do them justice. The beauty of mandibles and carapaces and perfect segmented limbs.

I'm glad my lab is at the edge of camp. I'd forgotten the excitement one feels in a forest. The sense that at any moment, something might emerge.

Five

Later

I told Birkenshaw I was too tired for supper and wanted to turn in early, but after he'd eaten he dropped by the lab and asked me to join him for a drink. He was disappointed when I declined, and I almost changed my mind. But I don't want him thinking we're going to be pals.

He's an archaeologist and I think the camp diplomat; the way he smoothed things over between Ridley and me at the airstrip; and yet there's something about him that makes me keep my distance. Maybe it's his habit of licking his very red lips.

He's plump, thirtyish, with a russet beard and Billy Bunter glasses, and that freckled skin which peels without going brown. His cut-glass diction evokes the era of cricket on the Green and honey still for tea. I'm not sure if it's genuine, or protective mimicry.

For a while he hung around and asked about my work. When I told him I study mantids, he didn't give the usual shudder, he was interested. 'As in praying mantises?'

'That's right.'

'Fascinating little fellows, aren't they?'

'Don't tell me you're an enthusiast?'

'Oh, I wouldn't say that.' He fingered a killing jar. 'I read somewhere that while they're screwing, the female bites off the male's head, and he keeps on plugging away. Is that true?'

'That's mostly in labs,' I said curtly. Why do laymen *always* mention that? I was glad when he left.

But something he said bothers me. He seems to think I'll be helping on the dig. I told him he's mistaken, I've got my own work to do, and he said not to worry, I can clear it up with the Professor in the morning. But it does make me wonder. This job rather fell into my lap, the Institute managed everything. 'Three months in the jungle,' they said. 'Just the ticket to help put things behind you.'

How come they arranged it so quickly? How much have they told Professor Atkinson? And was there was a *quid pro quo*?

Why did I automatically decline Birkenshaw's offer of a drink? Why have I always been alone?

It's not as though I can blame my parents, they're laughably normal: Father a bank manager, Mother a housewife. As a girl, Marjorie was a miniature version of Mother, embroidering 'guest towels' for her bottom drawer; now her daughters are doing the same. As for Edwin, he was horribly typical: Meccano and cigarette cards as a boy, rabid interest in the War – then dirty magazines under the bed and a yeasty smell of semen. He loathed me because I wasn't like him, I let down the side before his 'chums'.

When I was little he made my life a misery – *viz*, the

wasps' nest. Then one day when I was thirteen I realised I was taller than him. I took him aside and told him that if he touched my stick insects again I would kill him. He saw that I meant it, and never did.

How strange. What I thought was the 'black wall of the jungle' behind the heliconia is actually the upturned root disc of an enormous fallen tree. The roots rear higher than the roof of my lab, and the rest of the tree lies down the slope, its topmost branches in the river. It's a ceiba. Like the one we passed on the river.

Ceibas are sacred to the Yachikel; that's the name for the local Indians. I know this because Ridley just dropped by 'to check on me'. He says the tree outside my lab fell last year in a storm, but the Indians refused to chop it up and haul it away. 'Harming a ceiba,' he pontificated, 'is strictly taboo. The Yachikel name is *yaxché*, means 'green tree'.' God he went on, I couldn't shut him up. Even spelt it for me for Christ's sake, told me that in Mayan the 'x' is pronounced 'sh'. I wish I could get it through his pony-tailed head that I don't wish to *know* about his wretched Indians.

And dear Lord, how the man stinks. A noxious blend of cigarettes, unwashed male and mildew. Birkenshaw also smells of mildew, although not as much; he says that soon I will too. It's the humidity, one's clothes never really dry out.

It's curious that Ridley seems to revere everything about the Indians, and yet he cares nothing for the rainforest. To him it's merely a repository of threats. In the dugout he regaled me with the usual advice for those new to the tropics:

shake out your boots before putting them on; watch where you put your hands and feet; wear light-coloured clothes so that you can spot any nasties hitching a ride.

A few minutes ago he favoured me with a long list of creatures which are out to get me. Piranhas, caimans, electric eels, stingrays. Jaguars, peccaries (AKA wild pigs), scorpions, spiders, hornets, poisonous ants, snakes (the worst are pit vipers, all species are fearless and they come right into camp, one bite is fatal). Plus there's a host of ghastly diseases (does he think I don't know about malaria? I'm slathered in DEET!). My favourite deadly peril is a tiny fish called *candiru*. If you go for a swim it has an endearing habit of wriggling up your anus.

And he *loved* telling me about *boro* worms; I think he means the larvae of the bot fly, you get them from infected mosquito bites and the maggot burrows under your skin. Last month Ridley had one on his back. 'Carbuncle size of a golf ball,' he boasted. 'Had to get the Doc to burst it. Pulled out a worm as big as this.' He held up his little finger. 'And d'you know the most dangerous thing in the jungle?' he went on, knowing very well that I didn't. He pointed straight up. 'Trees. One of 'em falls on you, you're history.'

'Well, good luck to them,' I said tartly. 'We cut down too many as it is.' That shut him up. He didn't want another row.

I'm pretty sure I know why Ridley has buried himself in the jungle all these years. Something Birkenshaw said in the dugout made me wonder; then when we reached camp and Ridley and J.C. were unloading the gear, I saw him put his hand on the boy's back to steady him. He kept it there a fraction too long. The boy registered no expression, but for a moment Ridley's face was taut with longing.

If I'm right, it can't have been easy for him in England. On Friday nights, Edwin used to boast about going onto the Common with his 'chums' for a spot of queer-bashing.

I don't like Ridley and I don't share his predilections, but I feel sorry for him. Hopeless longing is something I know all about.

Two in the morning

Bloody Ridley, he's brought it all back. I can't stop thinking about Penelope. Not as I hallucinated her in San Cristóbal, but as I first saw her the night we met.

15th December 1972, the Institute Christmas party. Not even a year ago. Seems like another life. It had been a running joke ever since I'd joined the Institute that I never danced; the fun was in trying to force me. I didn't care. By then I'd grown an exoskeleton every bit as tough as those of my mantids. Only this year my chief tormentor was Rowbotham, and he wouldn't let up. Until Penelope came to my rescue.

'I should throw in the towel if I were you,' she told him, her cultivated tones carrying over the din. 'I don't think he wants to dance with you.'

People laughed, and Rowbotham put up his hands in mock surrender. 'Corbett, you've the luck of the devil!' he shouted over her head. 'If this one can't get you to dance, you're made of stone!'

She'd been facing him rather than me, and now she turned and tilted her head and smiled up at me. 'Don't worry, I shan't even try to persuade you.'

That smile. It set my ears ringing. My legs felt inordinately far from the floor. She wasn't a student, I'd never seen her before, she must be someone's girlfriend. So why was she talking to me?

She was too perfect to be real. She wore what she later described as 'her ethnic look', that floaty frock of celestial blue embroidered with the tiny mirrors and the butterflies. With every outbreath a little gap appeared between her neckline and the top of her breasts, and with every inhalation it was miraculously filled. I imagined that when she was getting dressed she'd simply slipped that frock over her head; a world away from my fat sister struggling into her elasticated girdle and her fortified bra to 'lift and separate' her wobbly, marked flesh.

She was still smiling up at me. 'Are you the Dr Corbett who teaches my brother?'

'I don't know,' I blurted out. 'Who's your brother?'

'Alexander Dale.'

I searched my memory and came up with a darkly handsome boy with no aptitude for science.

'Xander says you're a marvellous teacher. Incredibly patient.'

Her beauty was surreal, it was making me dizzy. Long glossy black hair hanging loose from a central parting, the way girls wear it these days. Dark-blue eyes as clear as glass, childishly full red mouth – and the palest, smoothest skin. She wasn't made of flesh, but of supple white porcelain. Snow White, I thought with a sensation of falling.

Later when she was leaving she asked me – *me* – to find her a taxi. As I opened the cab door I did something recklessly brave, I asked her to a concert.

For a moment she hesitated. Then she lifted her shoulders in the smallest of shrugs. 'Why not?' Drawing her coat closer about her. It was shaggy white sheepskin embroidered on the outside with flowers, and as a fleecy curl touched her cheek, something twisted painfully in my chest and I thought of that line in *Hamlet* about not letting the winds of heaven visit her face too roughly. I would do anything in the world to keep her from harm. I would kill anyone who hurt a hair of her head.

That's the truth. It's what I felt. Seeing those words now fills me with horror.

Six

I ought to turn in but my mind's buzzing.

It's been hours since camp settled for the night – though it's far from quiet. Generator juddering, the pulsing ring of frogs, shrieks and rustles from the jungle. And now and then from under the heliconia, a rapid deep knocking sound, I think it's a toad.

They call this a camp, but it's more like a small village. We're in a clearing on a slope about thirty yards up from the river. A dozen or so palm-thatched huts, the largest being the sleeping quarters and the 'Mess', that's where we eat. Each hut is dimly lit by lightbulbs dangling from the rafters. Between them are shadowy walkways shored up by logs and split bamboo.

The sun was going down as we arrived. I'd forgotten how suddenly it sets in the tropics; you can actually watch it sink. By then, two sleepless nights had caught up with me, and nothing seemed real. In a blur I was introduced to various grimy males: archaeologists, draughtsmen, photographers, cooks; a sozzled Mexican called Dr Mendoza, I think he's the camp medic. No sign of the Professor. But I was surprised to see two armed guards, villainous-looking *mestizos* with handlebar moustaches and real machine-guns. Birkenshaw says they're not here to keep hostile Indians out, but to guard the finds; apparently the black market in Maya art is doing a roaring trade.

The workmen on the dig are mostly Indians, but there aren't any in camp right now, they return to their village at night; it's downriver, we passed it on the way. I'm relieved about that. I don't like them. They make me uneasy. I don't know why.

There were Indians with us in the dugout. Two young women, two children and a baby, plus J.C., the handsome boy at the tiller.

'They're all Yachikel,' Ridley told me. 'Amazing people if you get to know them.'

The Indians in the dugout were smaller than the ones in San Cristóbal, scarcely over five feet. Flat, unsmiling mahogany faces and long unkempt black hair cut in a fringe across the forehead; I could hardly tell men from women. Some had dark triangles tattooed on their chins, and all were barefoot, the women and children in grubby calf-length shifts of unbleached calico, J.C. in shorts and a faded Superman T-shirt that was mostly holes. The baby was sick, its mother scarcely into her teens. Sunlight cast coppery glints in her infant's dark hair. It gazed at me dully, its wizened little face crusted with greenish snot.

In an undertone I asked Ridley why he admired them.

'Why wouldn't I? For one thing they've never been conquered. *Conquistadores* never even tried.'

'Sensible chaps,' remarked Birkenshaw. 'Ten feet of rain a year and a jungle full of poisonous snakes. Why risk that to conquer a few Indians?'

'But surely,' I said, 'that girl's much too young to be a mother?'

'The Yachikel do things differently,' Ridley said with a glance at Birkenshaw. 'The women grow crops and see to the children; the men hunt. They don't mix, except to mate. The men's bonds are with other men.'

Birkenshaw sniggered. 'Like the Greeks: a woman for progeny, a boy for pleasure.'

'Ignore him,' Ridley told me coldly.

We'd been going six hours when we came to tall cliffs the colour of dried blood, a narrow waterfall plummeting from the top. Ridley pointed past the cliffs at a gap in the jungle and the red gash of a path. 'Their village is through there.'

J.C. steered towards it, and soon afterwards the women and children scrambled nimbly up the muddy slope and vanished among the trees without a backwards glance.

Ridley explained that J.C. and the women are cousins. 'His uncle's the *akij*. Village shaman. You'll want to talk to him, he keeps a mantis in his hut. Helps him contact the spirits.'

No I bloody won't, I thought. I don't need help from some witch doctor, thank you very much.

I've realised why I find the Indians unsettling. I don't want their beliefs bleeding into my work. If they think they can contact the spirits, fine. But my beautiful mantids have nothing to do with that.

At the airstrip while we were waiting for the dugout, Ridley warned me how to conduct myself with the Ya-chikel. 'Don't look directly into their eyes, and don't try to shake hands.'

'Whyever not?' I said.

'They don't like it. Far as they're concerned, you might be an evil spirit or a ghost.' He shrugged, as if to excuse a foible, but I could tell that he was in earnest.

At the time I didn't think much of it, but now it strikes me as horrible. How could you live like that? The constant fear that anyone you meet might be a ghost?

Seven

Next morning

Macaws!

They woke me with ear-splitting squawks, and I scrambled out of my hammock in time to see six of them racing overhead, magical birds of ruby and sapphire, too enchanting to be real. My first wild macaws. According to the guards, they fly over camp every morning.

They brought tears to my eyes. Took me right back. That sad old macaw at the zoo when I was a boy, and Mother was trying to make me forget what Edwin had done to the wasps' nest. Poor Mother. She couldn't have known that I will hate my brother to my dying day for burning that nest.

It's 7 a.m., already stinking hot, cicadas rasping away. I've just walked a few hundred yards uphill to a rickety bamboo bridge spanning a little stream. I've seen my first leaf-cutter ants, a line of wobbly green fragments. They were worryingly close to the path. How do they avoid getting trampled?

Then, under the bridge, I caught an emerald flash. I thought it was only a lizard – *until it ran across the water on its hind legs.* A basilisk! Never thought I'd see one of those.

All of which makes up for a pretty lousy night. Camp was in darkness by the time I turned in, and I was glad of my torch. I share sleeping quarters with Ridley, Birkenshaw and two other archaeologists, Marshall and Watts. Everyone was snoring, but someone had set up my hammock and hung my mosquito net from a bamboo frame, and beside it they'd planted two stakes. Too exhausted to undress, I took off my boots, upended them on the stakes, unzipped the net and eased myself in.

I'm no stranger to hammocks, but I couldn't relax. Being cocooned in the mosquito net provided an illusion of safety, and yet I felt vulnerable, perhaps because the hut has no walls. All night I floated in darkness, around me a confused sense of movement, of shadowy comings and goings. That's doubtless because my hammock is near the path to the latrine.

At 4.30 a.m. I was jolted awake by unearthly roars. Flipping over, I made the classic beginner's mistake, damn near trapped myself in a winding sheet of hammock and net. My heart was hammering, and still the din went on. Primal, relentless. Intimidating.

Howler monkeys. Birkenshaw warned me last night that they roar at dusk and dawn, and also before bad weather. In other words, they roar a lot. I hope to God I get used to them. I don't like monkeys. Perhaps it's their similarity to human beings. Somehow I always think they should know better.

By five they'd shut up, and I fell asleep again until the macaws. Camp is empty now, everyone's up at the dig. Birkenshaw left a note pinned to my hammock, he's saved me some scraps in the Mess and will fetch me at nine. *Prof wants you up at the dig by 9.45. Be warned, it's a stiff climb.*

Damn and blast it to hell. Why can't I go off into the forest? I've already seen so many riches, and yet what surrounds camp is only *secondary* forest; a few years ago the Indians 'cleared' it for crops, then moved downriver and left it to grow back. The old-growth forest is further upriver. That's where I need to be.

I'd forgotten how much effort it takes to stay healthy in the tropics.

Ridley maintains that if you never wash, the mosquitoes eventually leave you alone, while Birkenshaw says one must wash every day. I'm with Birkenshaw. Someone left me a pail of river water and I used my coconut soap that's supposed to deter mosquitoes. I brushed my teeth with sterilised water, donned clean clothes, socks, freshly oiled boots, snake gaiters. Took my Paludrine, liberal spraying of DEET. Then realised I'd forgotten the sun-tan oil, so I had to smear that on and apply the DEET all over again.

I've had breakfast. 'Scraps' turned out to be a delicious mess of rice and beans with lime juice; also pawpaw, fried manioc, and a chocolate-brown fruit called *zapotes*, it's oversweet and tastes nothing like chocolate. The coffee's first-rate.

Only cooks and guards for company – and birds. Hummingbirds and little chattering yellow jobs with black eyestripes; a tiny black wren-like thing with a fetching vermilion head; and my first toucan, with a bright yellow bib and massive orange beak.

Birkenshaw's late. Come on, I want to get this over. I've a bad feeling about the Professor.

Fucking little martinet. I'm so angry I can hardly write, but I need to keep a record of our little spat in case there's a row with the Institute.

'The dig' is a series of seven terraces cut out of a precipitous green hillside above camp. A stiff climb indeed. We laboured up massive limestone steps, past piles of rubble smothered in bush. On each terrace Indians were hacking vines away from monumental stone blocks, many of which were blackened by fire and broken in pieces, as if they'd been flung down the slope.

'That's why they call this place Piedras Quemadas,' panted Birkenshaw. 'Means Burnt Stones. Whole settlement came to a sticky end around 700 AD.'

Professor Atkinson was waiting for us on the crown of the hill, standing like some latter-day potentate in front of an overgrown mound he grandly calls 'the Temple'. Behind him an imposing backdrop of forested mountains and deep-cut valleys, with here and there a giant ceiba rearing above the canopy. Below us the thatched roofs of camp and the coppery gleam of the river. On the other side, more forested mountains marching towards the horizon.

The Professor stood with legs braced and hands on hips, lord of all he surveyed. Stocky, tanned, khaki shirtsleeves rolled back to display muscular forearms matted with crisp black hair. A man's man, doubtless attractive to women. He reminded me of Professor Challenger in *The Lost World*.

A head shorter than me, he was making up for it by standing on a stone. Didn't waste precious time welcoming me, oh no. Just rapped out orders about helping on the dig.

I told him that wasn't possible, I had my own work to do. Whipping off his sunglasses, he gave me what he doubtless believes is a piercing stare. 'I repeat,' he said. 'Eight sharp every morning in the Mess. If I don't need you, you'll be free for the rest of the day.'

'What happens if I don't turn up?' I said mildly. 'You'll throw me in the brig?'

'I'll pretend I didn't hear that, Corbett. Come now, you're a Cambridge man, you know how things work. It can't be a surprise, your consulting duties are set out in the paperwork.'

Which of course I've never bothered to read.

'The Institute promised you'd help,' he went on. 'It's why I allowed you to come.' Something in his tone told me that he knows about Penelope.

A gaggle of silent Indians had downed tools to watch. Birkenshaw was squirming, Marshall and Watts clutching their clipboards. Ridley was grinning and puffing a cigarette.

'No need to sulk,' the Professor said curtly. 'I shan't be requiring you every day. If you stay with your guide, you can go wherever you like. From here to there.' He pointed first to his right, in the direction of the Indian village, then left to the eastern flank of the hill.

'That's secondary forest,' I snapped. 'No good to me, I need old-growth forest. Over there.' I pointed upriver.

'Out of the question,' barked the Professor.

'Why?'

'Because I say so.'

'Why?' I repeated.

He jabbed a finger at Ridley. 'You tell him, you're the Indian-lover.'

Birkenshaw repressed a snigger, which Ridley ignored. 'Upriver there are valleys where even our Indians won't go,' he told me. 'Too many spirits.'

'Oh come on,' I said.

'Last year a man was killed,' the Professor cut in. 'Take it from me, Corbett, not all Indians are friendly—'

'It wasn't Indians,' Ridley said quietly.

The Professor snorted. 'So who was it then, evil spirits? Point is, it caused no end of trouble and I won't have it again. Is that understood, Corbett? Upriver is *strictly out of bounds.*'

I opened my mouth to protest, but he spoke over me. 'The latest finds, please, Birkenshaw. Let's see what he makes of them.'

Birkenshaw produced a box of potsherds nestled in cotton wool and shoved them under my nose with a pleading glance: *Please, old chap, humour him, will you?*

The shards were sketchily daubed in reddish-brown, in a free-flowing style that struck me as oddly cartoonish. From a cursory glance I made out a scorpion, a jaguar and a fairly impressive leaf-nosed bat – but I decided to play dumb, said I didn't recognise anything except the jaguar.

The Professor bristled.

Birkenshaw tried to smooth things over. 'Jaguar's rather jolly, don't you think? Grinning like a Cheshire Cat?'

'It's not grinning,' I said impatiently. 'It's baring its teeth in a snarl.'

I knew at once that I'd shot myself in the foot.

The Professor gave a satisfied nod. 'Make a note of that, Birkenshaw. I knew it'd be useful to get a biologist's take. Right, chop, chop, everyone, back to work!'

You idiot, I told myself.

Birkenshaw was chuckling. 'Bad luck, old man. You've just justified your presence on the dig.'

At some point during my row with the Professor, I became aware that one of the Indians was staring at me. I think it was when I said I need to go upriver.

He was older than the rest, although with Indians it's hard to tell, and like the others he wore a grubby T-shirt and shorts. Scratches on his knees, blisters on his hands; they all have those, apparently the lime plaster on the stones burns their skin. But unlike the others, this man had two broad black bands tattooed on his wrists. The way he stared at me. Not hostile exactly. A sense of knowledge in his dark eyes which I found peculiarly intrusive. Unpleasant, even.

Afterwards I asked Ridley who he was. He hesitated. 'That's J.C.'s uncle. Name's Kayun. Bands on his wrists are the mark of the *akij*.'

So that's the village shaman. The one who keeps a mantis in his hut and can contact the dead. Or rather, he thinks he can.

Ridley wanted to know why I'd asked. I fobbed him off, but he wouldn't let it rest. 'He's not someone you want to talk to without me,' he warned.

'I've no intention of talking to him at all,' I said. 'Anyway, if he's a shaman, what's he doing on the dig?'

'Needs the money, of course. Though he only works

part-time. Four days here, three days off, doing his *akij* stuff. Taking *muktan*, that sort of thing.'

'And I suppose you're just dying to tell me what *muktan* is,' I said drily.

'Not much to tell. Secret concoction made from some plant. Helps him talk to the ancestors.'

'You don't actually believe that.'

He blew smoke out of the corner of his mouth. 'He's pretty convincing.'

'I'm surprised the Professor lets him work part-time. I wouldn't have thought he'd tolerate such nonsense.'

Again Ridley hesitated. 'It keeps the peace with the rest of them.' I got the sense that he was lying.

Why bother to lie? As if I care about his precious Indians.

Eight

We've had another downpour. Débris from the canopy clattering onto the roof of my lab, and in the distance the thump of a falling tree. Must have been a big one, it made the ground shake.

Lunch was soured by my row with the Professor, although fortunately the great man himself remained up at the dig. Ridley and Birkenshaw kept nagging me to fall into line, and I kept telling them it makes no sense. 'I'm an entomologist, for Christ's sake. You don't really think I can help on a dig?'

'That's not the point,' said Birkenshaw with his mouth full. 'He runs the show, and he wants you there.'

'But why? What does he stand to gain?'

'You heard him, a 'biologist's take'. He's always on the lookout to publish, maybe he thinks you can give him a leg-up over his rivals. You know how it works.'

'Well I'm damned if I'm going along with it.'

'Listen, Corbett,' said Ridley, lighting a cigarette. 'He knows he's a second-rate archaeologist and this is a second-rate dig.'

'Oh, steady on,' protested Birkenshaw.

Ridley ignored him and jabbed a grimy finger at me. 'You're a Cambridge man. The Prof's redbrick to the core. He's touchy. Especially now. Don't push his buttons.'

'Why especially now?' I said.

'Sidelined,' mumbled Birkenshaw. 'Big conference in Chiapas, he wasn't invited. Nose seriously out of joint.'

'So humour him,' said Ridley.

'Is that what you do?' I said.

He fingered his ponytail. 'I know him, Corbett. Butting heads won't work. As long as you don't openly question him, you can pretty much do what you like.'

'Including going upriver?' I said.

'Well obviously not that.'

'Whyever not? It can't really be because of some incident a year ago.'

'Got it in one,' snapped Ridley. 'The Prof is responsible for our safety. And as his right-hand man, so am I.'

'The man who died,' I said. 'Who was he?'

'Just some Indian,' said Birkenshaw.

Ridley looked at him with frank dislike.

I asked how he died. Ridley pretended not to hear, so I asked again. Frowning, he stubbed out his half-finished cigarette and lit another. 'We don't know. He went upstream and didn't come back. Few days later we found what was left.'

'What happened to him?'

'I told you, Corbett, we don't know. He was – mutilated. A lot of blood sprayed on the rocks.'

'Jaguar?'

'Oh, no. No animal would have done that.'

'You mean it was people?'

He hesitated, his face carefully blank. 'The Prof thinks it was other Indians. Or loggers, or *chicleros*.'

'What do you think?'

He blew out a thin stream of smoke. 'I've no idea.'

'But surely there was an investigation.'

Birkenshaw snorted. 'Out here?'

I said to Ridley, 'For someone who admires Indians, you seem remarkably incurious.'

His blotchy face went dark. 'Look. Corbett. I've lived with these people. I know when to stay out of their affairs.'

Soon afterwards we broke up. I've been in the lab ever since. I suspect there's a lot they're not telling me, but honestly, who cares about some dead Indian? I just wish the living ones would leave me alone.

Later

I've had a nap in my hammock and I'm feeling much better. I've worked things out. Ridley, the Professor, Kayun. It's all about money.

That story about the dead Indian: Ridley and the Professor cooked it up between them – or at least embellished it – to keep people in camp. They're trying to scare me. It makes sense when you think about it. Lowers the risk of expensive search parties, soaring insurance, that sort of thing. And who knows, maybe the Institute's had a word too. I can imagine the telexes flying back and forth. *Keep an eye on him will you? Don't let him wander off.*

As for that Indian – Kayun – he's also after money. Last night Birkenshaw told me that the Yachikel aren't above indulging in a little theatre if a boatload of tourists ventures as far as their village. As soon as they hear the outboard motor, the Indians shed their T-shirts and shorts for penis sheaths, and hide their Swiss Army knives and their steel saucepans. All to flog a few shoddy bows and arrows that couldn't hit a tree.

If they can lie to tourists, they can lie to us. Kayun can't contact the dead. It's just another lie to make money out of white men. That's what he saw when he stared at me. Money.

Well stuff that. I can handle him and I can handle the Professor. He's not the first little Hitler I've had to deal with in my career. I shall play along for the next few days, make him think he's won, that I'm toeing the line. Then I shall slip that boy J.C. a few *pesos* and we'll bloody well head upriver.

Nine

The way Kayun stared at me. As if he knew everything about me.

Maybe you're right after all, Dr Walker. Maybe writing it down will help. Let's see if it works.

People talk as if everyone falls in love in their lives but that's not true, for lots of us it never happens. It hadn't happened to me. I'd gone through school, National Service, a degree, a doctorate and years at the Institute without being attracted to anyone; nor had any female shown an interest in me – except once in the public library when I was eighteen, and a girl whispered to another that I had 'good shoulders'. Why 'good', I wondered. I thought I looked like a coat hanger. But I hoarded that remark for years.

First love at forty-two. It was like falling off a cliff. I'd been alone all my life – and suddenly I wasn't.

The week after the Christmas party I took Penelope to the concert. Late Beethoven? What was I *thinking*? I caught her swallowing a yawn, and as we were leaving I said sorry.

She gave a forthright snort. 'Not your fault I'm thick. My Pa adores that stuff.'

Her father, I thought. Is that how she sees me?

That night she was wearing a mini-dress patterned in psychedelic orange and pink, with knee-high boots of shiny green vinyl. I gently intimated that I preferred the butterfly frock, and she shrugged, said she was trying out different looks.

As I was walking her to the Tube, she said she'd finished a course at something called 'Lucy Clayton'. 'God it was a hoot! They taught us how to get out of a car without showing one's slip!' She'd just started a part-time job in a boutique on Parson's Green. 'Like Biba, only not so grand. Although' – that enchanting smile – 'I don't suppose you've heard of Biba.' She'd also begun a part-time job at the Institute, two days a week in the Bursar's office; she said her brother kept teasing her for trying to be a career girl. I don't think I said a word. I was too busy looking at her.

I knew she was utterly out of my league. Too young, too posh, too beautiful. I didn't care.

Next day I took the Tube to Parson's Green, found the boutique where she worked, and asked her out for coffee. For an instant she hesitated; then she gave her adorable little shrug and said OK. I should have known then that she was only going along with things. But *why*? That's what I've never been able to work out.

We went to a Wimpy Bar across the Green, and afterwards we said goodbye under a birch tree. It became 'our tree'. That's when I got the talisman.

Back at the Institute I studied my reflection in the Men's

Room mirror and my spirits sank. Bony, loose-limbed, a tall man's stoop. Brown hair cut unfashionably short, hooked nose, dingy deep-set eyes, prominent Adam's apple. I was ridiculous. Of *course* she didn't want to be with me.

So why say yes to a second coffee, and a third? Why smile and put her hand on my arm? Why tell me I had a gorgeous husky voice, I should be on the radio?

I see-sawed between elation – She loves me, we're made for each other – and howling despair – She's only being kind. Putting up with me for her brother's sake.

At last I understood why poets and pop singers bleat endlessly of love. I was experiencing all the clichés for myself. I couldn't eat, work, sleep. Watching her emerge from the boutique I felt breathless and light-headed. Love *hurt*, it actually hurt. I was connected to her by an invisible thread stitched to my heart, and at every turn of her mood I felt its tug.

She told me everyone called her Penny, but I never did, I insisted on Penelope. I loved the feel of the syllables in my mouth, like sun-warmed pebbles. I loved that the name evoked Ancient Greece – as did her surname, Dale, like Arcadia. It made me think of white marble, unattainably pure. Everything about her was perfect. Her name. The butterflies.

We were meant to be.

Our second coffee nearly didn't happen because when I dropped by the Bursar's office some beatnik was chatting her up. Long greasy hair and a moustache, Army fatigues, combat boots. Who did he think he was, Che Guevara?

Before when I'd seen her in the Bursar's office she'd been

demure in a twin-set and midi-skirt, but today she too wore camouflage gear and clumpy boots; her eyes were ringed with kohl, her hair was scraped back. 'Your beautiful hair,' I protested. She rolled her eyes. 'I'm thinking of having it chopped off. Like Mia Farrow in *Rosemary's Baby*.'

At Christmas she went home to her parents for a fortnight. I didn't have her phone number, it was torture. The week after New Year she asked me not to drop by the Bursar's office any more. She said things at the boutique were 'frantic', and she only had time for a rushed third coffee.

The following week she let me buy her dinner at a restaurant near the boutique. It was my first encounter with Italian food: we had pizza pie and red wine in a bottle covered in straw, I felt madly 'with it'. She looked stunning, in a mauve Empire-line frock, her hair piled up (I prayed this meant that Che Guevara was out of the picture). Over coffee I gave her the present I'd bought: a silk scarf from a terrifyingly up-market shop in Knightsbridge.

To my horror she wouldn't accept it. 'Oh Simon, no,' she said in dismay.

My world tilted. 'Don't you like it?' I stammered.

'It's not that. It's far too expensive.'

'Nothing's too expensive for you.'

'No. Simon. You can't do this.'

I gave an incredulous laugh. 'But I want to! The shop where I bought it, it's named after a Greek god! That's how I knew it was perfect. Hermes, he's the—'

'Hermès,' she said distractedly, making it sound French.

I kept on at her and in the end she slid the box into her bag. The way she said thank you: so formal. I found that chilling.

As I was putting her in a taxi, desperation overcame me and I took her in my arms. For an instant she tensed; then she relaxed in a beautiful gesture of surrender and tilted back her head and regarded me without expression.

I've never experienced anything as wonderful as that kiss. They say kisses are sweet and it's true, she really did taste of honey. And her neck was so soft, she smelt like strawberries.

All too soon she was pulling away, giving my shoulder a little pat. 'Thank you for a lovely evening,' she said politely, without meeting my eyes. 'Goodbye, Simon.'

Why 'Goodbye'? I agonised on my way home. Why not 'Goodnight'?

Answer: Because she doesn't want to see you again. Because it's over. *Finis*. The End.

Why didn't I realise? Why couldn't I leave her alone?

Ten

Yesterday I decided to toe the line for a few days. Be a good boy and help out on the dig. Well forget that. After what just happened I'm damned if I'm going up there again.

At breakfast the Professor told me to take a look at the 'stelae'; they're like huge stone pillars covered in carvings. I'd slept through the howler monkeys and was feeling much better, so I said all right, and off we went up the hill: Ridley, Birkenshaw and I.

We'd reached the massive stone steps leading from the second terrace to the third when I noticed what they actually were. Each monumental limestone slab was resting on the back of a naked stone man. He was bigger than life-size, kneeling with his arms wrenched painfully behind him and his wrists tied to his ankles, his chest pressed against his thighs, his defeated Indian face squashed against the step beneath. I counted twelve stone steps crushing twelve stone captives.

'Human sacrifice,' Ridley muttered. 'Blood to appease the gods.'

Birkenshaw pouted his wet red lips. 'We don't know that

for sure.' Then to me: 'The Maya believed you could only reach heaven if you died a violent death.'

'But not if you were sacrificed,' said Ridley. 'You're not telling me these poor sods thought they'd go to heaven.'

'We don't know,' repeated Birkenshaw sententiously.

'Well it all sounds charming,' I said to shut them up.

On the next terrace Birkenshaw pointed out a line of carvings on a wall. Some were of animals, rather well-observed. I made out a toad shedding its skin, and a loathsome little spider monkey, its scrawny prick poking up between its legs. But what I thought was a tadpole turned out to be a man's gouged-out eye, dangling down his cheek on its squiggly optic nerve.

'They were into mutilation,' said Ridley, following my gaze.

'They didn't see it like that,' Birkenshaw said tartly.

'How do you know?' mocked Ridley.

As we climbed higher, they went on telling me things I didn't want to hear, while sniping at each other, like two schoolboys scrapping in front of the master. Birkenshaw seems genuinely fascinated by the ancient Maya, although he regards their descendants with genial contempt, and won't countenance any connection between the two. Ridley, the ageing hippie, regards the Yachikel as the Maya's 'spiritual descendants'. He thinks this makes them special. I think it makes them savages.

According to my guidebook the ancient Maya were a peaceful lot, sort of philosopher-priests, charting the heavens from their hilltop temples; but from what I learnt today that's totally out of date. Soon after the War, some Americans stumbled across a series of wall paintings not far from here, and that changed everything. Torture, decapitation, self-mutilation: you name it, those wall paintings show it. I wonder if the picture in that woman's book on the plane came from there. The priest attacking his own penis with a knife.

By the time we'd reached the fifth terrace I'd seen enough. Archaeologists can 'clear' this site all they like. They can divide it into neat little grids, and draw diagrams, and number their 'finds' – but they can't tidy away what's underneath. People were slaughtered here. They were maimed, eyes gouged, hearts cut out. This hillside is soaked in blood.

The stelae we'd come to see were in pieces, having been hurled from above during some battle a thousand years ago – which doubtless resulted in lots more trussed and mutilated captives. Every surface of every fragment was covered in orderly rows of squares, each one filled with carvings of bewildering complexity. They were done in the same weirdly modern style as the potsherds I saw yesterday. 'As if they were doodled by a drunken cartoonist,' I remarked.

Birkenshaw looked offended. 'It's writing.' He indicated a carved hand with three drops falling between finger and thumb. 'That means *chok*. To scatter. This one's *tzak*: to invoke.'

'Don't tell me,' I said sourly. 'More human sacrifice.'

'You guessed it,' said Ridley. 'Sometimes they even did it to themselves.'

'I wish you wouldn't exaggerate,' snapped Birkenshaw. 'There's no evidence of ritual suicide, that's pure conjecture.'

'Makes sense, though, doesn't it?' said Ridley. 'If violent

death gets you to hobnob with the gods, why not take a short cut and top yourself?'

Birkenshaw rolled his eyes at me. 'Our Ridley has a lively imagination. He forgets he's not actually an archaeologist. What we're talking about here is blood-letting.'

'Well it was pretty extreme,' said Ridley. 'Women pushing a stingray barb through their tongues? Men did it to a different part of their anatomy.'

'I know about that,' I muttered.

'In fact, only the nobles went in for it,' Birkenshaw said testily. 'They sprinkled the blood on paper – yes, Corbett, they had paper, and books – then they burnt it to conjure the spirits.'

'Yachikel still do,' said Ridley. 'But don't worry, Corbett, these days they use dogs' blood.'

'I'm not worried,' I said. 'All this has nothing to do with me.'

Birkenshaw turned pink. 'I'd have thought you'd want to know something about them. After all, you'll be here for three months.'

'Yes, but not on the dig. I do have my own work, you know. Now what is it you want me to see?'

Birkenshaw adjusted his Billy Bunter glasses. He indicated another part of the stela and launched into some explanation of what it was supposed to depict.

That's when I stopped listening. I'd spotted a wall a few feet behind us. Like the stelae it was covered in carvings; but these were different. Striding across the stone, almost life-size, was a grinning skeleton. No, not exactly a skeleton, its belly was obscenely swollen and pockmarked. And in one bony fist it clutched, by a tuft of hair, a severed head.

That head. It was so very dead. Tongue lolling from cold dead lips. Eyes shut with such finality. They would never open again. Never, never, never.

'What's that?' I croaked, pointing at the thing on the wall.

'Ah,' said Ridley. 'Meet Kisim. Death god. One of many. Also called The Flatulent One.'

'It's revolting,' I said.

'He's meant to be.' Birkenshaw was defensive. 'The blotches and the swollen belly indicate a state of advanced decay. The Maya were realists, they noticed everything.'

Ridley drew on his cigarette. 'Our friend Kisim lives in the underworld. Xibalba. The Place of Fear. Another name for him is Flying Scab.'

Dark spots were swimming before my eyes. I stared at the skull's grin that was no grin. At the swollen belly blotched with decay.

I thought, She has been in the ground for six months. This is what she has become.

Our dinner in the Italian restaurant was on the 16th of January. After that came three months of awfulness when she was avoiding me, I won't go into that. By April I was at my wits' end, so I wrote her a letter.

I posted it on the Thursday and I know from Jacintha's testimony that Penelope got it the next day when she came home from the boutique. I also know that minutes afterwards she threw a few things in a bag and drove off to her parents in Cheltenham. And that she was frightened and upset. Because of me.

It was the week before Easter. Dark, a hard frost. Ice

on the roads. She overtook too fast on the brow of a hill. The coroner said the lorry driver was lucky to survive. He commended the police for advising the family not to view the body, and when he asked the clerk to hand round the photographs of the accident scene he warned any relatives present that they'd do better not to look. Soon afterwards he delivered his verdict: Accident.

But was it? Or was it because of me that she took that bend too fast?

If it hadn't been for me, would she still be alive?

Since Cambridge I've jotted the hours I've worked every day in a notebook, along with any important events which have occurred. In the weeks after she died, I noted nothing. Then the night before the inquest I took a marker pen and drew a thick black line down each page. I didn't need to write what it meant. I will never forget.

I've realised that in this journal I've stopped recording dates. It wasn't deliberate, it simply happened. But now I realise why. I don't want to know what day it is, because if I did, I'd have to count back and know that it's been X days since she died, then X+1, and so on and so on, each day a stepping stone taking me further away from her.

Sometimes I think I'm getting better. Like yesterday with the macaws and the lizard that runs on water. Then something happens – like coming face to face with that horrible rotting god – and once again I'm a million miles down in the darkness, all contact broken for ever.

I will never see her again. Never, never, never.

I can't bear it. I would do anything to bring her back.

Eleven

Night

It wasn't her. I wanted it to be her but it wasn't. I know that now.

I had left that horrible carving on the fifth terrace in a rush, telling the others I felt sick. They offered to come down with me to camp, but I told them I could manage on my own. As I was crossing the bridge the basilisk once again shot across the stream. I'm told it does this every time someone passes. Poor little thing spends its life being frightened out of its wits.

I didn't fancy talking, so I grabbed lunch before the others returned to camp. My brush with the Maya had left me feeling soiled. All that violence and mutilation. Their putrid god of death.

On leaving the Mess, I spotted J.C. As I'd anticipated, the boy was quite prepared to flout the rules for a few *pesos*, and we swiftly agreed terms to go upriver tomorrow. He didn't seem too bothered about those valleys that belong to the spirits.

In the afternoon I took a nap. I woke thick-headed and

bleary. I went to my lab and sorted my gear, ready for an early start. I located that toad who's been making a racket at night. He lives under the heliconia, a big brown cane toad like a creature in a fairy tale. *Bufo marinus*: I've named him Bufo. His warty skin exudes a poison that deters predators. It also causes hallucinations, like L.S.D.; in one of Birkenshaw's books it says that the Maya may have used it in their rites. For all I know, that Kayun fellow does too. If he can't get *muktan*.

Stop putting it off, Simon. Get it down on paper. Then you'll see that you're making something out of nothing.

Shortly before five o'clock I decided to climb the hill again. I told myself that I needed to go up there to spy out the land for tomorrow's illicit foray upriver, but deep down I knew I was climbing it because of Penelope.

'She will always be alive in your heart,' Dr Walker told me once. 'She lives on in your memory.' That made me almost blind with rage. 'What you say has no meaning!' I shouted. 'My heart is a lump of muscle! My memory is a network of electrical impulses in my brain! *She isn't there!*'

She isn't there. She isn't anywhere.

But what if I'm wrong? What if something of her does still exist?

That's why I climbed the hill. To summon her.

Summon. Conjure. Invoke. Whatever it takes to bring back the dead.

The Indians had already left the dig as I made my way uphill. They always leave well before sunset; apparently they're scared of their ancestors' ghosts.

No such concerns for us Westerners, of course.

Birkenshaw, Marshall and Watts were on the fourth terrace, the Professor and Ridley on the crown of the hill. I
spotted them above me, deep in talk; when they saw me
they moved round to the other side of the 'Temple'. I was
glad about that, I didn't want them spying on me.

The fifth terrace was deserted, apart from that ghastly
stone skeleton on its wall. I averted my eyes as I picked my
way around the mounds of cut vegetation. I could tell from
their smell that they were already starting to rot.

At the edge of the terrace I found a burnt fragment of
stela by a clump of dieffenbachia. It felt wrong to sit on the
stone itself, so I sat on a boulder beside it, facing upriver –
having hastily checked for fire ants and snakes. I dumped
my rucksack at my feet, then unzipped my breast pocket
and took out the talisman. Carefully I unwrapped it and
laid it on its white handkerchief on the blackened stela. I
looked down at her hair wound around the twig. I wanted
to touch it, but I dared not. Lying on the stela, it seemed
charged with power.

That was why I'd climbed the hill: out of some confused,
irrational notion that when I summoned her I had to do it
here, in this sacred place.

I didn't have much time. In half an hour the sun would
set, and ten minutes later it would be dark. Already the
frogs had started their monotonous piping. The forest ech-
oed with cries and shrieks.

The howlers began their monstrous, grating roar. In the
failing light it sounded eerie. Unnatural.

A hot breeze stirred the dieffenbachia. I've always disliked the plant. The pale blotches on its leaves make it seem
diseased. In Jamaica they call it 'dumb-cane' because a

drop of sap in the mouth of a rebellious slave would cause hours of choking pain. I bet the Maya used it on their captives. From the sound of them it's what they'd do.

The howlers fell silent. A flock of parakeets sped screeching across the sky. I watched a silk moth settle on the handkerchief, close to the talisman. I made out its feathery antennae, the delicate pearl and russet markings on its wings. I wondered why people think butterflies are more beautiful than moths.

Then, in the dust not far from my feet, I spotted a dead bird. Same species as the one I saw yesterday, beautiful little thing the size of a wren. Velvety black body, bright vermilion head. It was quite untouched, nothing to show how it died. Still warm. Limp. Perfect.

Somehow it brought a lump to my throat. My eyes ached. I ground my fist against my boulder. Clenching my jaws, I bit back the grief until my head felt about to explode. No breaking down now, Simon. No disgusting blubbery sobs.

'P-Penelope,' I stammered. 'Are you there? Are you anywhere? Come to me – *please*! Tell me – say you forgive me! Please I can't bear it.'

Tears were streaming down my cheeks. I was choking and gasping, clamping my jaws, baring my teeth. Pleading with her to come back.

Suddenly, without warning, a violent wind was sweeping across the hillside. It came from upriver, rushing, whirling, flattening the dumb-cane, flinging dust in my eyes. It was a sign, it had to be. I hardly dared believe it. She had heard me.

As suddenly as it had come, the wind died. Behind me a dove flew off with a clatter of wings, making me gasp.

After that – silence. Even the frogs had gone quiet. The dumb-cane stood utterly still.

That's when I sensed it. A presence. Beside me on the stela. I stopped breathing. Didn't dare turn my head. What if she had come to my call? How could I bear it?

'Penelope,' I whispered, still without turning my head. 'Is it you? Are you here?'

Still the silence went on.

At last I summoned my courage. I turned to look. No one there. Of course not. I had willed myself to feel something – anything – to fill this aching void, when the truth was, nothing had happened. No one had come.

A bat flickered past my head. The frogs resumed their piping. Beside me on the stela the moth was gone. I could barely make out the talisman, except by contrast. The handkerchief showed pale in the gloom.

Crying had left me drained. I wiped my eyes on my sleeve. Fumbled in my rucksack for another handkerchief and blew my nose. Then I picked up the talisman – my last link with Penelope – and wrapped it up and zipped it back in the pocket of my shirt.

On the terrace below, Birkenshaw was waving at me and shouting my name.

I don't know how long I remained on the fifth terrace, but by the time I made my way down to the fourth, it was dark and everyone had gone.

An overcast night, I had to use my torch, and somehow I missed the path to the bridge. I was still on *a* path but it wasn't the right one. I was lost.

The jungle pressed in on me, alive with screeches and

rustlings. I placed my feet warily, on the lookout for snakes. I was unpleasantly aware that I'd forgotten my machete, and that my rucksack contained only binoculars, notebook, water bottle and DEET. Not much use in an emergency.

God it was a relief when I found the bridge. Moments later my torch beam caught the saturnine features of the guard as I stumbled into camp. I could have kissed him.

I'm prevaricating again. What Birkenshaw told me at supper means *nothing*, but it shook me, I can't deny that. He says he saw someone sitting beside me on the stela.

It was noisy in the Mess and I thought I'd misheard him, so I asked him to repeat what he'd said. He told me he'd seen J.C. sitting next to me. He'd assumed we were making arrangements for the boy to be my guide.

I shook my head. 'There was no one with me, I was alone.' Birkenshaw didn't hear me, he was busy stuffing his face. 'What did they look like?' I said, struggling to keep my voice level.

'What?' he mumbled through a mouthful of *enchilada*.

'The person beside me. What did they look like?'

'Like J.C., of course.'

'J.C. wasn't there.'

'Yes he was, he was right beside you, sitting on the stela – which he oughtn't to have been, that's why I was shouting.'

I sucked in my lips. 'Try to remember what they looked like.'

He stared at me, wiped his mouth on the back of his hand. 'I don't know, Corbett, like an Indian. Small, long black hair. It was too dark to see his face, I just assumed it was J.C.'

'So – it could have been a woman.'

He sniggered. 'Not likely, old chap, no women on site – worse luck!'

'There was no one there,' I repeated.

He patted my shoulder. 'Not to worry, old man. These Indians come and go like cats. Let's have another beer.'

For a moment when he told me, my heart gave a painful jerk and I actually thought it was her. I thought: it worked. I summoned her and she came.

Then reason returned. Birkenshaw's right, it was a soft-footed Indian and I didn't notice because I was crying. Moaning and bleating about Penelope.

I'm ashamed of myself. Angry too, for believing – even for a moment – that she had come back.

Something else. Even though I know that what I did up there – messing about with the talisman, 'summoning' her spirit – I know it's all nonsense – but I rather wish I hadn't done it. And part of me is relieved that it *didn't* work.

Because when I think about it, would I really, truly, want her to come back?

On the one hand, yes. On the other hand – no. God, no, a thousand times no.

So it turns out that when it comes to these things, I'm just the same as everyone else. I find the idea of a spirit – a revenant – all right, a ghost – I find that terrifying.

Besides. If she did come back, she would be angry.

Twelve

I never told you what happened, Dr Walker, and I'm not sure I ever will. So perhaps this journal is only for me.

Two days after we had dinner in the restaurant I went to the boutique and Penelope wasn't there. 'She doesn't want to see you,' said her friend Jacintha who worked there too, a fat young blonde with an ugly red slash of a mouth.

Same thing happened when I collared Xander after class. 'I don't know, Dr Corbett,' he said sulkily. 'She just doesn't.'

'But *why*? What have I done?'

'I don't know.' Scuffing the lino with his plimsole, his black hair hiding his face.

She wasn't in the Bursar's office. They said she'd chucked in her job. I never saw her at the Institute again.

The word 'obsession' comes from the Latin *obsidere*: to besiege. That's how it felt, as if I'd been taken over by someone else: someone who invaded my dreams, my every waking moment with images of her. My thoughts circled endlessly. She *must* have feelings for me or she wouldn't have agreed to the coffees, or dinner. Therefore I must have done something wrong. Therefore if I could talk to her, I could make it all right.

I rang the boutique but Jacintha told me not to call again. The seventh time I rang she sneered. 'We had a laugh about that scarf of yours, Penny and I. She called it 'old-lady chic'. Gave it to her grandmamma.' The bitch was lying. Penelope would never say that.

I knew she shared a flat with Xander, so I went through every Dale in the telephone directory. They weren't listed. Eventually I sneaked into the Bursar's office after hours and found the number in the files. I managed a few halting words before she cut the connection.

If only I could see her in person, tell her to her face how much I loved her. Then she would understand, she would realise we were meant to be together.

For eight days she stayed away from the boutique. On the ninth she returned. I waited under our tree until she left work. She gasped when she saw me, actually gasped. Stammered that the whole thing had been a mistake, *please* leave her alone – then ran all the way to the Tube.

I was horrified. I'd blundered again. Jumping out from behind a tree? What were you *thinking*? Of course she was frightened! Poor girl simply needs more time.

For two weeks I kept out of sight. Skipped classes, couldn't work except to slink to the lab and feed my mantids. I told myself that for now it was enough to stand on the Green and breathe the same air she did: an act of devotion, of purest love.

I was convinced she hadn't spotted me on my lonely vigils – until a letter arrived at my flat. Thick ivory paper headed with three embossed columns of partners' names, and below them a single paragraph in icy legalese, threatening proceedings if I did not 'desist'. I was appalled. I vowed never to contact her again.

I managed it for six weeks. I got through my work barely functioning, like a robot. At first I reasoned that if I thought about her constantly I might get sick of her. It didn't work. I tried the opposite, total suppression. That didn't work either. I couldn't manage not to think about her for more than a few minutes.

Then one morning I forced myself to go to the Natural History Museum to check some specimens, and as I was leaving I saw her getting into a taxi on the Cromwell Road. Now tell me, Dr Walker, what are the odds of that in a city of over seven million people? How *could* it have been by chance? I hailed a cab and told the driver to follow. Like in a film.

Her taxi pulled up in Chelsea outside an imposing Edwardian mansion block. I told my cabbie to park a hundred yards down the street. I *never* meant her to see me – but she did. Slammed the door of her cab and stalked towards me.

My driver gave a low whistle. 'Now you're for it, mate.'

She stood with her arms crossed while I rolled down the window. Her face was set. Such freezing anger. Such contempt. 'This has to *stop*,' she said. 'You seem to have concocted some ridiculous fantasy about me. Get this through your head: I am not Penelope, I am Penny. I like fashion, the Rolling Stones and boys my own age. I detest insects. They give me the creeps. So do you. I don't ever want to see you again. Is that clear? Don't ever contact me again.'

Then she walked back up the street and into the mansion block.

Once again I'd frightened her. Her anger was like the startle response of a female mantid, rearing up and spreading her wings to confront a predator. Was that how she saw me? A predator?

Next morning two policemen came to see me in my office. They were actually quite nice, and let me off with a caution. I don't think they'd even have bothered if her father hadn't been something in the City.

The moment they'd gone I went to Professor Cartwright, made a full confession and tendered my resignation. To my astonishment he burst out laughing. Called me a 'sly dog', said I wasn't the first chap to lose his head over a pretty face, and what did these girls expect when they wore skirts up to their navels? He told me to take a fortnight's leave till the dust settled.

I ended up taking three weeks. It was horrible. Holed up in my flat, pacing, subsisting on Vesta curries and boil-in-the-bag cod. I didn't even open the curtains.

Why couldn't I stop loving her? Why couldn't it be like my boyhood crushes on film stars, which at the time had felt overwhelming – until suddenly they weren't, and the face of my then beloved was merely a face, all magic gone? Why couldn't that happen with Penelope? Why couldn't this terrible affliction come to an end?

But not in the way that it did. Oh God, not like that.

Once during my purdah Jeremy came round and I told him what had happened. He said I had to give her up. I said, 'Would you ever, *ever* give up Wanda over a simple misunderstanding?'

He said, 'But Wanda and I, that's different. The first time I met her I knew she was the one for me.'

'So did I when I saw Penelope!' I shouted. 'Why does that make you a romantic, and me deluded?'

'Because – because, Wanda feels the same about me. And Penny doesn't.'

'Then why did she go out with me?'

'I don't know! Curiosity? Boredom? Maybe she's a bit of a prick-tease?'

I punched him. Well, my fist only grazed his chin, but it shocked us both. I said sorry and he said apology accepted, and soon afterwards he left.

More evidence that I'd turned into someone else. I am a talented scientist, I told myself. A good teacher, an authority on predation strategies of arboreal mantids. I am not a man who importunes women and punches my best friend. That is not who I am.

But it was. I'd uncovered a side of myself I never knew existed. And I missed Penelope dreadfully, it was shredding me inside.

Eventually I couldn't bear it so I wrote her the letter. Seven lines saying sorry for putting you through this, I swear I will never contact you again.

Why did I write it? Was it really to say sorry? Or was I trying to maintain a connection, even though she'd left me in no doubt that that was the last thing she wanted?

People say it's no use crying over spilt milk, but try stopping yourself, Dr Walker. Try 'putting it out of your mind' when you've caused irreparable harm. See how far you get.

Thirteen

For God's sake, Simon, pull yourself together.

I've just re-read the last few pages of this journal. All that pointless guilt, that bleating about Penelope. It won't do. The truth is I'll never know if I played a part in her death and it does no good to dwell on it. I need to stop thinking about her. I've put an elastic band around what I've written so far, to prevent me even catching sight of her name.

Get down to work. That's the ticket. The next three months are a golden opportunity. Publication, tenure – this is your chance. Thank heavens I arranged things yesterday with J.C. He's meeting me at eight with a dugout, a quiet one without a motor. We're going to slip away upriver.

He's friendly enough and speaks surprisingly good English; doesn't seem the slightest bit worried about venturing into the forbidden forest. Perhaps his Uncle Kayun has given him a charm to ward off spirits. Or more likely his illustrious relation is simply keen on the pesos our little jaunt will bring in.

It turns out that 'J.C.' stands for Juan-Carlos, although he says he prefers J.C. I asked if he has a Yachikel name too, but he didn't seem to understand; or maybe he'd rather not say. He appears to be rather good at polite avoidance – *viz* the night we arrived at camp, when he calmly moved out of Ridley's reach. He's half my age and it shows in his hands, they're as smooth and innocent as a child's: except for the blisters from the dig. I've given him a tube of calamine lotion for those. He seemed pleased.

Intelligent too, I showed him a photo of a mantid, which he recognised at once. Knows quite a lot about them, says they're good hunters, clever at hiding. I think we're going to get along fine. I hope so. He's my passport to the old-growth forest. Who knows what I'll find?

Excellent first day – though as yet no mantids. But give them time.

Leaving camp was easier than I'd dared hope, despite a near miss with the Professor. I was passing the Mess laden with gear when I bumped into him, but to my relief he barely noticed me. Ridley was with him and they were deep in talk with their visitor, a Mexican who arrived last night. According to Birkenshaw he's from some Foundation they're hoping to milk for funds. They're certainly giving him the VIP treatment, he's even staying in the Professor's own sleeping quarters.

J.C. was waiting at the river with a small dugout without a motor and we slipped away unobserved and paddled upstream. Half an hour later he veered left up a muddy little tributary overhung with trees. It wasn't even marked on my map. I loved that, it felt as if we'd paddled off the edge of the world.

Another forty minutes and we hauled up onto a narrow

stretch of reddish sand. I could hardly see it for butterflies, thousands of blue and orange daggerwings feeding on the salts in animal tracks; they rose in a shimmering cloud at our approach. J.C. secured the dugout, then found a peccary trail and I followed him into the deep green shadow.

Oh, I was right to hold out for the old-growth forest! It's utterly different from the secondary jungle around camp. Cooler, darker, the trees taller, undergrowth less rampant. I heard the screech and clatter of parrots. I breathed a swampy scent of earth and growth and decay. A weight lifted from my shoulders.

Craning my neck, I saw a dizzying mosaic of emerald leaves fretted with black branches, strange fruits and nameless flowers. I tried to picture its inhabitants gnawing, perching, scrambling, hiding, hunting – all just out of sight. Then the sun went in and the canopy darkened almost to black.

We didn't use our machetes, instead J.C. cut a switch of bamboo for himself, and one for me. Soon afterwards he showed me what it was for when he casually flicked a three-foot coral snake off the trail.

'Was it poisonous?' I said as calmly as I could.

He broke into a grin that lit up his handsome face. 'Oh yes, but they're cowards. Only bite if you tread on them.'

I've read about Indian woodcraft but I've always dismissed it as a cliché: the myth of the Noble Savage. There's nothing noble about J.C. in his tatty blue shorts, but I must admit I was impressed. Barefoot and bare-chested, his skin the colour of earth, he moved with silent ease despite his heavy load of fogging gear, scrutinising his surroundings constantly, noticing everything.

He showed me the undersides of leaves darkened by thousands of tiny fig wasps. He placed a fat, glossy millipede on my palm; I chuckled as I felt the light dry patter of its feet. By a stream he took a stick and gently coaxed a tarantula from its burrow. We exchanged grins as we watched the magnificent creature retreat inside. And once he politely stopped me from putting my hand on a branch. Next moment I saw it too, a huge black ant almost as big as my thumb. Its bite would have given me hours of intense pain; hence its name, bullet ant.

J.C. doesn't use binoculars and he has the hearing of a bat. Once he signed me to silence, whispering that he could hear birds fleeing from a troupe of howlers coming our way. I couldn't hear a thing, but sure enough a few minutes later a horde of the formidable shaggy brown monkeys was ransacking the canopy above our heads, and around us bush crickets were raining down into the leaf litter. They were diving for safety; monkeys eat them like crisps.

I envy J.C. He's part of the forest in a way I can never be.

So thinking about it now, it strikes me as odd – even a little suspicious – that on a day-long hike he couldn't find a single ceiba.

Next day

I hope I'm not going to have a problem with J.C. This morning I showed him a photo of a ceiba in my field guide, I said we need to find one because I study the mantids that live on them.

As he looked at the picture his face went still. 'We don't

hurt these trees,' he said softly. With his flat Roman nose and chiselled lips he was as inscrutable as a Maya carving.

'That's fine,' I reassured him. 'I don't need to hurt them.' Briefly I explained about fogging. I mimed pumping the aspirator and puffing clouds of pyrethrin into the canopy, then collecting the arthropods that fall onto the sheets spread out below.

He nodded slowly. 'And the things that fall – what happens to them?'

'I take them back to camp and identify them.'

'Are they dead?'

'That's what fogging does. But it doesn't hurt the tree.'

He looked at me in puzzlement. I don't think he understood.

Today at least he did find me ceibas. In fact he found three. Trouble is, I couldn't fog a single one.

The first we came across was a giant, it made the trees I'd studied in Jamaica seem like saplings. I stood in the hollow between two of its great buttressed roots, craning my neck at its outstretched arms a hundred and fifty feet above my head, a dizzying world of vines, bromeliads, ferns, orchids. In a nearby copal tree I spotted a flock of green and blue parakeets and a toucan squabbling over mistletoe berries, but in the ceiba there were no birds. I put my hand on its trunk, between cone-shaped spikes six inches long. An armoured tree. If it fell on me I'd be impaled fifty times over.

I told J.C. to unpack the fogging gear, but to my irritation he said no, not this tree: spider monkeys up there. I couldn't hear any monkeys – until suddenly they erupted with jeering hoots and started pelting us with sticks.

J.C. pulled me out of range, narrowly saving me from

being spattered with dung. He was laughing. 'They don't like us under their tree!'

'All right, you win,' I said with a sheepish grin. 'We'll find another tree.'

We did, but we couldn't fog it either, this time because of bats: a line of furry brown blobs on the trunk, hanging nose-to-feet about twenty feet up.

The third tree harboured a macaws' nesting-hole, so high up I needed binoculars. The thought that I might have inadvertently poisoned a clutch of chicks made me go hot and cold with horror.

By now I was beginning to suspect that J.C. was doing it on purpose. *You want ceibas, fine I'll show you ceibas. But only those you can't fog.*

I've no idea if he's protecting ceibas *per se*, or whether he objects to fogging in general, or even to my presence in the old-growth forest. If I asked him I doubt that he'd tell me. He doesn't need to. He is simply taking unobtrusive yet highly effective steps to thwart my work.

I had trouble like this in Jamaica. The locals there call ceibas 'duppy trees', they say they're the haunt of ghosts. I had the devil of a time persuading anyone to help me, but it paid off in the end. I found the grizzled mantids that got me the job at the Institute.

I'm damned if I'm going to back down now.

Fourteen

Who the hell does Ridley think he is? J.C. must have said something about fogging the ceibas because Mr Bloody Indian-lover has just had a go at me in the lab.

'Listen,' he said, breathing cigarette fumes in my face. 'If you want to go upriver that's your funeral. But I won't have you making trouble with my Indians.'

'I'm not,' I said.

'Blowing poison at their sacred trees? What d'you call that?'

'Science,' I replied. 'And it doesn't hurt the tree, it only kills what's living in it.'

'No Yachikel would see the difference. To them it's the same thing.'

'Well that's their lookout.'

'No, it's mine if it makes trouble on the dig. I've told you, to them the ceiba is *yaxché*, green tree, centre of their world. They'll happily cut down a centuries-old mahogany and flog it for the price of a few saucepans, but they'll never fell a ceiba.'

'And I told you, fogging doesn't hurt the tree.'

'Try telling them that!'

I leant back in my chair and crossed my arms. He was genuinely angry, his blotchy face had gone puce. I thought this excessive; I wondered if he was jealous of my time in the forest with J.C. I watched him grind his cigarette under his heel and make an effort to control himself. 'Why does it have to be a ceiba?' he growled. 'Why not a rubber tree or a copal?'

'Because the mantids I'm after live on ceibas.'

'J.C. says you haven't found any mantids.'

'Because I haven't fogged any ceibas!'

That's as far as we got. He could see that I wasn't backing down; although before he left he made one last attempt. 'Why not ask Kayun? He knows about mantids, he'll find you masses in no time.'

I laughed. 'What, in between getting high on plant alkaloids and communing with spirits? No thanks, I think I'll stick to science.'

And honestly, it's a bit rich of Ridley to make a fuss about a few trees just because they matter to his precious Indians – when up at the dig he has them happily 'clearing' whole swathes of jungle. At least my fogging leaves the trees alive. And the insects come back, I know they do, I've seen it happen.

It's not as if I *like* fogging. The first time I did it I felt like a murderer: all those little lives. But I've made my peace with it. A few individuals have to die for the sake of the species. And I never fog more trees than I need.

One good thing, though. With all this fuss about fogging, I've hardly thought about Penelope.

*

That was three days ago. Since then I've fogged three ceibas. Take that, Ridley.

Each time I reaped a rich harvest of spiders, ants, beetles, barklice, tree-hoppers, butterflies, assassin bugs, owl-
flies, caterpillars, frogs – you name it. But not a single
mantis. Just one empty egg-case as delicate as origami, and
a nymph's moulted exoskeleton: a translucent, mocking
phantom of what I seek.

After I'd fogged each tree, J.C. watched without expression as arthropods and frogs pattered onto the sheets.
He's helping because he needs the money, he has a mother
and three sisters in the village; but he emanates mute resistance. And the evening after we fogged the first tree, I
found the tube of calamine lotion I'd given him lying on
my desk. I'll admit that hurt. From someone as politely inscrutable as J.C. it felt like a slap in the face. I'll also admit
that I like the boy and I want him to like me. But it can't
be helped.

And despite what Ridley says, I'm not aware that the Indians have made any trouble on the dig. They haven't said
anything to me either, although I do sense the same un-
spoken resistance as with J.C. No, it's more than resistance.
It feels as if they believe that I've transgressed.

Oddly enough, I felt something similar in the jungle
today. As J.C. and I were making our way back to the dugout, we came to a clearing created by a fallen tree. A stand
of bamboo had sprung up in the gap, and a vicious tangle
of cat's claw vines; the mass of vegetation barred our way
to the river like a magic thicket in a fairy tale. We had
to make a lengthy detour around it and by the time we

reached the dugout it was getting dark. That thicket almost felt as if the jungle were against me.

And later, as J.C. was paddling us back to camp, my torch caught the red eyeshine of a caiman on the bank. The beast was only five feet from the dugout: huge, like a dragon, its ridged grey-green bulk melding uncannily with the mud. As we glided past, its ancient eye met mine, and I had the strangest feeling that it knew what I'd done to those ceibas. I glanced back in time to see it slide into the river out of sight, a sinister ripple in the glassy black water.

But I can't *help* it that I fogged those ceibas. This is my work, it's what I came for. I have no choice.

No choice. I wish I didn't have this irrational feeling that in some way I was fated to do this. That it's inevitable.

First the caiman, now this. An odd little incident, hardly worth recording, but it's preventing me from turning in.

I was tired and I'd left supper early. Our sleeping quarters were empty, everyone still in the Mess. So why was my hammock violently rocking, as if someone had only just left?

Mindful of spider monkeys, I checked the pouch I keep tied to the head of the hammock, but it was undisturbed and still contained my necessaries for the night: torch, water bottle, DEET, toilet paper, knife. So not a monkey, then.

And it didn't *feel* like a monkey. For a moment, as I approached my hammock, I had the same prickling sensation I'd had on the fifth terrace after I'd 'summoned' Penelope. A presence. Very close. Not friendly.

Then abruptly the feeling was gone. I was surprised to find that I'd been holding my breath.

It *must* have been a spider monkey. I've seen lots of them near the Mess. Brazen little buggers, steal anything they can.

Blast them to hell. I'm exhausted but I can't sleep. So here I am, still in the lab.

Why no mantids? It's not natural. This is the Mexican rainforest, for heaven's sake, no shortage of insects! As I write, several doomed moths are circling the lightbulb above my head and the floor is littered with dead ones; there should be mantids among them, they're also drawn to the light. So why don't they come?

I miss them.

I remember the first time I ever encountered one. Summer in Grenoble, it was after lunch and I was walking back to the lab when I spotted a sizeable insect in a bush. Until then I'd never thought much about mantids, only seen them in books. But as I bent over the elegant little creature it reared up and spread its gauzy green wings, threatening me with both forelegs raised, like a miniature boxer. I was enchanted. For the first time ever I peered into that fascinating triangular face: those bulbous, wide-set, alien eyes. Carefully I picked up my prize and carried it to my office, where I spent the rest of the day observing it. One of the happiest days of my life.

Why do I love them? Let me count the ways.

For that extraordinary head and the human-like way in which it turns to look.

For their courage in facing off predators ten times their size.

For their uncanny ability to hide in plain sight.

Their tireless patience in waiting for prey.

Their spiny, murderous forelimbs which they uphold as if in prayer – until the moment they snap shut on their luckless victim with unbelievable speed.

For their willingness to hunt anything: insects, spiders, frogs, reptiles, even mice and birds.

For the mysteries of their existence, which we have yet to fathom. What do they see? Is it true that they can't hear? How do they know the precise moment to attack?

But maybe the real reason I love them is that they live their lives alone. For the mantis, life is solitary.

Mantids have always been special. In China they symbolise fearlessness. The Greeks thought they pointed the way home for lost travellers. The Ancient Egyptians worshipped a mantis god who led the souls of the dead to the underworld.

The Yachikel also think they're messengers from the dead. That's why that fellow Kayun keeps one in his hut.

I saw him today in the Mess. I was at the Westerners' table, he was with the Indians. I suppose he's been on my mind because of the ceibas, and that's why I chanced to look his way. It gave me a jolt to find that he was watching me.

Unlike the other Indians he has no fringe; his long dark hair hangs straight from a central parting. No telling how old he is, that weathered brown face could be anything between forty and sixty. No beard, none of the Indians has; although unlike them, he sports a wispy moustache. It lends him a rakish air.

His eyes are small, black and very deep-set. As I met his gaze he inclined his head and gave me a wry smile which I found peculiarly unpleasant. Not that it conveyed hostility. What I disliked was his assurance – I might almost say *familiarity*. As if he knows everything about me.

In short, the fellow gives me the creeps. And I wish I'd never heard of that plant he uses in his rites. *Muktan?* I want nothing to do with him and his filthy potions for contacting the dead.

I *will* have nothing to do with him.

11.30 p.m.

I'm still shaking. It's quite hard to write.

I was finishing up in the lab. A downpour had just ended, rain dripping steadily off the eaves, frogs noisily piping, and from the heliconia came Bufo's rapid deep knocking; he'd been at it so long I hardly heard.

I'd decided to move my desk around to face the other way. I don't like looking at the root disc of the fallen ceiba, it feels like another silent reproach. I'd just finished re-arranging things and was sitting at my desk when I realised that Bufo had fallen silent. The frogs had stopped too. The night was utterly still, apart from the drip drip of rain falling from the eaves.

That's when I got the unmistakeable feeling that I wasn't alone. I glanced behind me. No one there. Switched on my torch and raked the heliconia with the beam. Still nothing. But my heart was thumping, all senses on edge.

Then something made me look down and I saw it, a finger's breadth from my right boot. A monstrous snake. It had to be eight feet long. I saw its sinister flat triangular head. The telltale black diamonds on its flanks. Pit viper.

Ridley was right, the creature had no fear. It neither coiled to strike, nor slithered away. It simply stared at me. Its eyes were a sulphurous yellow, the pupils vertical slits of fathomless black.

Time stretched. It seemed like hours before the viper slid into the darkness beneath the heliconia. I tried to follow it with my torchlight but I lost it. I *think* I saw it slip beyond the ceiba's roots but I'm not sure. I hate the idea that it might still be there.

A close encounter with a venomous snake is enough to shake anyone. But there's more to it than that. I know it's irrational, but I swear that the creature looked at me with knowledge.

I know what you did.

Fifteen

I had a rotten night and the dream is still with me.

I was in the jungle and I was frightened. I knew she was coming. I heard branches thrust aside and a rustling of leaves. I tried to run but my feet were sunk in earth. Then there she was, blocking my escape. A thing of charred skin and crumbling bones. Half her scalp was ripped away and her belly was obscenely swollen, pregnant with a rotting foetus. She came towards me with open arms.

I started up with a cry. Luckily, the howler monkeys were beginning their pre-dawn roar; the others attributed my outburst to that.

I dared not go back to sleep, so I've taken refuge in the lab. I've washed, dressed, dabbed iodine on my bites (the one in the crook of my elbow is itching like mad). The birds are making a din, which is helping a bit. Doves cooing a lament, kiskadees chattering. They're the yellow ones with the bandit eye-stripes. Cheeky little sods, into everything.

It's no good, I have to write down the rest. I will never show this journal to anyone now. This is for me, to get it out of my head. And for you too, Penelope. It's always for you.

When I heard she was dead I was petrified the police would come after me. Maybe they'd found the letter, or someone had heard something and I'd be arrested for importuning her; or summoned to explain myself at the inquest.

When nothing happened I was relieved – and also crushed. I was nothing to do with her. I didn't matter.

I can't delude myself that she didn't read my letter because at the inquest Jacintha said she did. Xander had gone away for the weekend and Jacintha was staying at their flat because of some problem where she lived. She'd left the boutique early, I can't remember why, and was watching TV when Penelope arrived. All Jacintha remembered was that Penelope opened a letter from 'some admirer' and seemed 'a bit upset'. She said Penelope put the letter down the waste disposal, then flung a few things in a bag, called out that she was going to her parents, and left. Jacintha didn't know who the letter was from. She said Penelope had lots of admirers, 'always some man drooling over her'. The coroner had no more questions and soon afterwards he gave his verdict.

Throughout the hearing I'd sat in the back row with my hat pulled low and my scarf over mouth and nose; no one gave me a second glance. Everyone was bundled up because of the cold weather; plus the heating in the courtroom was on the blink. I'd seen Xander taking a seat at the front beside an elegant couple I took to be the parents: a handsome silver-haired man, a slender woman in a blonde fur coat. I glimpsed her face before she sat down, it was drawn and unseeing, as if none of this was real. On Xander's other side was the beatnik who'd chatted up Penelope in the Bursar's office. He'd had a haircut and looked much younger. His eyes were red-rimmed from crying.

No one recognised me, but I felt as if they did. I felt as if I had a sign around my neck: I KILLED HER.

Jeremy once said that even if my letter did upset her – even if it contributed in some way to the accident – I never *meant* it to happen, so I shouldn't blame myself. Nice try, Jeremy. But it doesn't matter what I intended. It's the effect that counts.

And of course, Jeremy doesn't know the rest.

Penelope arrived at the flat that night at 5.53 p.m. I know because I saw her. She didn't see me, I was in the mews opposite the mansion block. I was waiting there because I felt dreadful about the letter and I wanted to make sure she was all right.

Which of course is another lie. I went because I had to see her.

I watched her hurry down the steps with a navy leather vanity case and a Dickins & Jones carrier bag. It was dark, and under the streetlamps I saw the pale glimmer of her white sheepskin coat. I followed her to an underground car park a few streets away.

The car park was almost empty; presumably everyone had left for the weekend. Her red Mini Minor was parked in a shadowy corner. As I drew closer she flung her bags in the back and wrenched open the driver's door. I was on the passenger side of the car, and through the window I saw the litter on the seat: sweet wrappers, cassette tapes out of their cases, a dog-eared A to Z. On the dashboard lay a postcard of some Renaissance painting, a Nativity I think.

'Penelope,' I said gently.

She gave a start. No it was more than that, her whole body tensed. '*Christ!*' she gasped. 'Fucking *Christ!*' Rigid, she faced me. Her shoulders were up to her ears, her eyes black holes in her chalk-white face.

'Penelope – please. I just want—'

'Get away from me! Why can't you fucking leave me alone!'

I don't remember how it happened, but next thing I knew I'd gone round to her side and was trying to reason with her and she was attempting to get in the car and I was grabbing her shoulder. Not hard, I swear it wasn't hard, but she screamed as if I'd hurt her and we struggled briefly, then she broke away and got in the car and slammed the door. As she was reversing she scraped the car against a pillar, a dreadful metallic screech. Then she was speeding up the ramp, out of sight. The last thing I heard was the squeal of her tyres as she drove off.

At the inquest I was petrified that someone had seen us, or heard something, maybe a security guard, but no one had. And of course the scratches on her car would have been destroyed in the fire.

When the coroner gave his verdict and I knew I was in the clear, the relief was overwhelming. Then came the scalding wash of shame. Despicable. To be worried about myself.

If Jeremy knew what happened in the car park, he would probably still insist that I wasn't to blame. He would say that I can't possibly know how upset she was. Maybe she shrugged it off. Pretty girl like that, it wouldn't be the first time she'd had to fend off an over-eager admirer.

I've tried telling myself that. It never works. I saw how her hands shook as she struggled to reverse. I saw her bloodless face and her staring eyes.

I did it. I killed her. I caused that twisted wreckage. That blackened thing behind the wheel.

Sixteen

I thought I'd feel better after getting it down on paper, but I feel worse. And it's not helping that the mantids are staying away. I've been here nearly a fortnight and still not a single one. If I go back to England with nothing, I'm finished. No tenure and probably no job. So. I've swallowed my pride. Tomorrow I'm going to see Kayun and ask for help.

The man's a fake. I wish to God I'd never seen him.

J.C. took Ridley and me downriver in his dugout, and Birkenshaw came 'for the ride'. Ridley didn't want him to come, but Birkenshaw insisted. He seemed in high spirits, almost defiant. J.C. gave him a flat look I couldn't read.

Surprisingly, Ridley was on edge, smoking furiously and tying and re-tying his ponytail. Before we even left camp he warned me to treat Kayun with respect.

'I will if he will,' I said, remembering the Indian's over-familiar smile.

'Just humour him, will you?' said Ridley. 'He believes he's descended from the ancient Maya: the Lords of Piedras Quemadas. Bear that in mind.'

'What does he make of you digging it up?'

'Doesn't like it of course.'

'So why does he work there?'

He hesitated. 'He needs the money. Which reminds me, you'll need to take cash and gifts. I stocked up in San C., you can buy some off me.'

That's why my rucksack was crammed with disposable lighters, packets of safety pins, a canister of salt and two bottles of Johnnie Walker. None of which came cheap; doubtless Ridley made a healthy profit. And I couldn't help commenting on the whisky. 'Is giving them alcohol a good idea?'

'Kayun doesn't drink,' he said impatiently. 'He uses it for *akij* stuff.'

I laughed. 'Pull the other one!'

The village turned out to be a dismal huddle of palm-thatched huts a few minutes' climb from the river. Behind it lay a clearing where the Indians grow maize, beans, yucca and tobacco. In the dust in front of the huts, children and dogs played listlessly, while a girl knelt at a stone slab grinding maize. In the men's hut they lolled in hammocks, puffing on home-made cigars ten inches long. J.C. ambled over and they greeted him in Yachikel, ignoring us Westerners.

Ridley jiggled a bag of sweets and the children came running. With their grubby shifts and shaggy hair I couldn't tell boys from girls. I noticed that two had extra fingers, another a bad squint. Ridley had warned me about this, he said there's a high incidence of deformities as there are so few Yachikel left. 'Because we killed them all,' he said bluntly.

The girl grinding maize was the same one who'd been with us in the dugout on my first day; her baby slept beside her, tightly swaddled. I smiled at her and she gave me an unblinking stare. I don't know if that was because of the ceibas, or if she didn't recognise me. Perhaps to her, all Westerners look alike.

Two little girls emerged from the clearing, bent double under conical baskets of maize held in place by straps across their foreheads. They emptied their loads beside the girl with the baby, then plodded back to the clearing.

'Kayun's wives,' said Ridley. 'He likes them young.'

Birkenshaw sniggered and waggled his fingers at us in farewell. 'Toodle-oo, chaps!' Still giggling, he started after the girls, making a detour to avoid the one with the baby. J.C. and the men watched him without expression.

Ridley noticed my disgust. 'Haven't you rumbled his Billy Bunter act yet? He's another one who likes them young.'

'Don't you care?' I said.

'Look. If the Yachikel don't mind, I don't. It's their custom to take wives before they reach puberty.'

'So that makes it OK for Birkenshaw to rape children?'

He didn't reply. We were heading for Kayun's hut, which stood apart from the others behind a stand of dumb-cane and rattlesnake plant. 'Let me do the talking,' he said curtly, stubbing out his cigarette. 'I need a chat with him first in Yachikel.'

'Doesn't he speak English?'

'When he wants to. But don't get your hopes up, if he's on *muktan* he won't see us at all. And even if he does, he may just give you the usual rubbish he gives tourists. Whiff of copal incense, tell your fortune from your birthday.'

'Or what?'

'Or something more authentic.' He turned to face me. 'One other thing. The man who was killed upriver last year. That was his brother. He was an *akij* too. We don't talk about him.'

I stopped. 'Is that why Kayun takes *muktan*?'

'What?'

'To contact his brother. Find out who killed him.'

He made to reply, but the great man had emerged from behind the dumb-cane and was motioning us inside.

His hut was the usual thatched roof on posts; no walls, earth floor slippery with palm fronds. A net hammock hung at the back, and hunched beside it on a perch was a scarlet macaw. With an ear-splitting screech it half-spread its astonishing wings and began to preen. I couldn't repress a twinge of envy. Those wings weren't clipped, nor was the bird tethered to its perch. It stayed because it wanted to.

In the middle of the hut a low bamboo table was laden with what I took to be the tools of Kayun's trade. A small grindstone, bundles of dried leaves; four little animal figures woven from palm fibre: I made out a frog, a cat, a bird and a snake. A wooden dish was piled with blue glass marbles like the ones Edwin and I used to play with at school. And propped behind that was a wooden cross choked with orchids – white, orange, pale green – intertwined with garish red plastic tulips. From this floral concoction came a sweetish smell that was tantalisingly familiar. I still can't place it.

The exchange in Yachikel was brief and Ridley did most

of the talking, the Indian interjecting the odd word in a soft monotone. He seemed in charge, Ridley almost propitiating. At the end Ridley handed him a sizeable wad of bank notes.

'What was that about?' I asked under my breath.

'Nothing that concerns you,' Ridley replied. 'You're in luck, he's agreed to talk to you.'

Apparently the great man wasn't planning on taking *muktan* today, hence his willingness to grant me an audience – provided that I paid. He took my gifts without thanks and stowed them with Ridley's cash in a PVC Lufthansa bag slung over his shoulder; then seated himself on the floor beside the table and with a lordly gesture indicated that we should sit before him.

He'd swapped the T-shirt and shorts he wears on the dig for a grubby calico shift which he tented over his knees. Its frayed sleeves ended at his elbows, displaying an outsize chrome wristwatch that hung loose on his scrawny forearm. The tattooed black bands on both wrists proclaimed his status as a shaman, and on a thong around his neck hung a spike of sharpened bone; I guessed that was for blood-letting.

He looked furtive and seedy, and I regretted my decision to come. He was also in no hurry to begin. Puffing on his home-made cigar, he shrouded us in vile-smelling smoke and regarded me calmly through slitted eyes.

I noticed that the hand holding the cigar was missing the third and fourth fingers. 'He hacked them off himself,' Ridley murmured in my ear. 'Part of his initiation as an *akij*. He wants twenty pesos.'

'Twenty?' I whispered. 'Isn't that a bit steep?'

'D'you want his help or not?'

Reluctantly I handed over the money. The Indian took it, again without thanks, and stashed it in the Lufthansa bag. 'We will eat,' he told Ridley in English. 'Then I'll tell him what he wants.'

I bridled. 'You don't know what I want.'

He favoured me with his over-familiar smile. 'Kayun knows. First *ts'ul* must eat with Kayun.'

Oh, spare me the cod-native drivel, I thought. Out loud, I asked Ridley what *ts'ul* meant.

'Outsider. That's you and me.'

The Indian clapped his hands and a very young girl came in bearing three gourds of maize porridge and a dish of golden-brown tortillas. She set a gourd before each of us and the others fell to, scooping their porridge with scraps of tortilla. My tortilla was delicious, but the porridge was a tasteless sludge; I picked at it with my camping spoon. This elicited a scornful snort from Kayun, who made a comment to Ridley in Yachikel.

'He asks if you like the tortilla.'

I said it was fine. Kayun's reply made Ridley wince. 'He says it was made specially for you. A blend of maize flour and ground ceiba seeds.'

My turn to snort. 'How thoughtful. Tell him I didn't hurt his precious trees.'

The Indian regarded me through a haze of smoke. He ignored the young girl when she took away our bowls, then said to me, 'When her breasts grow, she will be Kayun's wife.'

The child couldn't have been more than ten, and I didn't hide my disgust. Kayun scratched his balls and leered at me. *You like them young too*, his black eyes said. As if he knew about Penelope.

Again the girl had been and gone, leaving three smaller gourds, each half-full of an unappetising cloudy yellow liquid.

'*Balché*,' muttered Ridley. 'Tree bark fermented with honey. You need to drink some.' He took a swig from his gourd and ostentatiously smacked his lips.

The stuff tasted innocuous, if slightly soapy. I managed a couple of mouthfuls.

After draining his gourd, Kayun jammed his cigar between his teeth and set a wooden dish on the floor before him, then filled it with water from a jug. He tossed in salt from the canister I'd given him and stirred it with his maimed hand. From a calico bag he poured a small pile of yellow maize kernels onto the floor beside the dish.

'This is good,' breathed Ridley. 'You're not getting the tourist treatment.'

The Indian put another handful of maize on the floor beside the first; these kernels were the colour of rust. Next came dirty white ones, then blue-black.

When this charade had gone on for long enough I said, 'I'm looking for mantids.'

The Indian ignored me, counting kernels of each colour and putting them together in a fifth pile.

'Mantids,' I repeated. 'Like the one on that roof post to your left.'

Kayun chuckled. 'Not many *ts'ul* notice that.'

'Notice what?' Ridley was annoyed.

'*Callimantis antillarum*,' I snapped. 'I spotted it as soon as we came in.'

She was perfectly camouflaged and looked for all the world like a couple of furled green leaves snagged on the post. Again I felt that twinge of envy. Why should she come to him and not to me?

She was ignoring the moth which had come to rest within striking distance on her post, because it wasn't moving. Her attention was fixed on the fly which had alighted before her; I could tell she was assessing the possibilities. When it happened, the strike was so fast I hardly saw it. One moment the fly was cleaning its forelimbs. The next it was struggling in those interlocking spines that would never let go.

People used to believe that mantids invariably decapitate their prey, but in fact they simply start eating whichever part is nearest their jaws. This means that they often eat their prey alive – as she was doing now, methodically nibbling the juicy flight muscles of the thorax. Eating their prey alive has given mantids a bad name. Although why it should I'll never know, when lions and other 'top predators' happily chomp on their living, struggling prey; but that's what the TV programmes always leave out.

Ridley nudged me in the ribs and I dragged my gaze away. Kayun had scooped up the multi-coloured kernels from the fifth pile and was tossing them in the water. He counted those which floated; then nodded, as if they confirmed what he already knew. Sitting back, he met my eyes. 'Your spirit is sick.'

It was so banal I nearly laughed. 'And how d'you work that out?' I said pleasantly.

He studied me with scornful pity, as if I were a retarded child. 'Listen, *ts'ul*. It's this way. In the world there are two nights. There's the darkness that everyone sees. It comes when the sun goes down. And there's the second darkness, the one underneath. Kayun sees both at the same time. He flies as a macaw. He walks as a jaguar. As a snake he enters the cave under the earth and hears the screams of the wind being born.'

Yes that's all very gnomic and poetic, I thought angrily. Out loud, I said, 'And I suppose you see all this when you take *muktan*?'

He hawked and spat. '*Muktan* is not for *ts'ul*.'

'What makes you think I want your filthy *muktan*?'

'Steady, Corbett,' muttered Ridley.

'You want it,' said Kayun. 'It's why you're here.'

'No it's not. I told you, I'm looking for mantids.'

He shot me a look of startling coldness. 'You poison our trees. That's why they stay away. That's why the *nayacan* comes.'

'I don't know what that means.'

Ridley stirred. 'Pit viper. I didn't know you'd had a brush with one.'

How the hell did Kayun know? I haven't told a soul.

'The *nayacan* sees you, *ts'ul*. It knows what you did.'

The *Callimantis* had finished eating, she was running her forelegs through her mandibles to clean them. After that she would groom her beautiful slanted eyes and settle down to wait for more prey, aloof in her soundless world.

Mantis, I thought, from the Greek for soothsayer. My head was spinning. That *balché* must be stronger than I'd thought. 'I'm looking for mantids,' I repeated.

'That is not why you came,' Kayun declared. He leant towards me. The whites of his eyes were yellow. I caught his reek of tobacco and rank male flesh. 'It is beside you,' he said distinctly. 'And you don't see.'

My skin prickled. I felt the hairs on my arms standing up. 'What is beside me?' I said hoarsely.

He bared his teeth in a grin. 'You know.' He spoke in Yachikel to Ridley, who frowned. 'He says, "It was beside you at *Xayaxché* too." *Xayaxché*, that's their name for Piedras Quemadas.'

I couldn't breathe. 'You mean at the dig? Something was beside me at the dig? Tell me, you bastard!'

Ridley put a hand on my shoulder but I shook him off. Kayun was still grinning. I wanted to kill him. 'This is a trick!' I burst out, lurching to my feet. 'You're quite the psychologist, aren't you? You spotted I'm unhappy and you bloody well took adv—'

'I don't need tricks,' the wretch cut in. 'You need to give it blood or it'll always be angry.'

'You fucking fake!' I shouted.

He broke into a neighing laugh and dismissed me with a wave of his maimed hand. 'Watch out, *ts'ul*. It's beside you!'

He was still laughing as I stumbled out of the hut.

Seventeen

Is he a fake? Or is there something in it? How could he know about that pit viper when I haven't told a soul?

She is beside you.

No, that's not what he said, he said '*it*'. But did he mean 'she'? Or is that what he *wants* me to think?

Ridley was angry with me for offending Kayun, he didn't speak till we'd reached the dugout and were preparing to head back to camp. 'You have no idea how much trouble you've caused,' he fumed.

'Then why don't you tell me?' I retorted.

He chucked me a paddle. 'Put your back into it. The current's strong.'

He and J.C. paddled in the bow. I was next, and Birkenshaw slumped behind me, snoring in a post-coital nap. I was still shaken by my encounter with that wretch, my hands trembling so hard I nearly dropped my paddle overboard.

'So what was all that about?' Ridley said over his shoulder.

'Mind games,' I muttered. 'Because I fogged his bloody trees.'

'You handled him all wrong.'

'And I suppose he was politeness itself.'

We paddled in silence. Then he said, 'I'd have thought you'd find something to admire in him. You being a biologist.'

'What's that got to do with it?'

'Closeness to Nature, that sort of thing.'

I forced a laugh. 'The man lives in a jungle, he doesn't have much choice.'

'It's deeper than that, Corbett. They believe everything has a spirit. Animals, rocks, trees, even insects. It's a different way of living.'

'Screwing children is certainly different.'

He tossed his head.

'Why are you so desperate not to make a judgement?' I said.

'Why do I have to?'

'But surely you have an opinion? I mean, you don't actually believe the man can turn into a jaguar? Or a bird, or a snake?'

'No, but he does.' He chucked his cigarette overboard.

Mid-afternoon, the air quivering with heat. Swallows dipping and darting over the water, butterflies rising from sandbanks in flurries of amethyst and topaz. On a dead tree a snakebird twisted its long black neck and watched me pass.

I said, 'Just because the man talks in non sequiturs doesn't make him wiser than the rest of us.'

He glanced at me. 'He really got to you, didn't he?'

'Isn't that his job? Sniffing out people's weaknesses.'

Playing on their hopes. *It is beside you.* How dare he?

And how did he know? Or was it merely native shrewdness, plus the odd snippet of information relayed by J.C.?

Who, I suddenly realised, had been listening to me denigrate his uncle.

Our paddles clashed and I said sorry. The boy nodded, unsmiling and remote.

In the village he'd shown a ruthless side I didn't know he had. After the children had gobbled Ridley's sweets, one of them, a tiny filthy creature about six years old, kept pestering J.C. to play. Eventually he gave in. Hoisting the child above his head, he carried it to a tree and told it to take hold of a branch. The child clutched one and J.C. walked away, leaving it stranded seven feet above the ground, clinging on for dear life and squealing in fright. After a while a woman ambled over and rescued it. It didn't go near J.C. again.

Behind me Birkenshaw grunted in his sleep. His shirt had ridden up, revealing a freckled paunch matted with russet hair. Ridley glanced at him in distaste. 'Yachikel believe each of us has an animal spirit companion. I've always thought his must be a peccary.'

'What's Kayun's?' I said.

'A powerful *akij* has several.'

'So it's official, is it? The man's a shape-shifter?'

'I only said he believes he is.'

'Does he need *muktan* to do it?'

He didn't reply. We'd run up against a floating tree and he was watching J.C. disentangle us from the branches.

In an undertone I asked Ridley if he'd ever tried the stuff himself.

'Once,' he said distantly. 'Years ago.'

'What was it like?'

J.C. wasn't wearing his T-shirt and as he leant over, Ridley's eyes stayed on his muscular brown back. 'It was extraordinary,' he said. 'The sense of – connection.' He flushed, shook his head. 'I don't mean sex.'

'What, then?'

J.C. freed us and we resumed paddling.

'I'll tell you one thing,' Ridley said in a brisk tone. 'It made me sick as a dog. Once was enough.'

'What's it made of?' I asked casually.

'I don't know, some flower that grows on trees.' He twisted round and gave me his knowing grin. 'Nice try, Corbett. And don't even think about asking the Indians, they never tell outsiders.'

'How come they let you take it?'

'Never you mind.'

Anyway, what makes Ridley think I want the bloody stuff? That *balché* was enough for me.

Later

I've just been down to the river again. In the sunlight it was greyish-green, but under the trees it was black, no knowing what lay beneath. Near the dugouts I found a dead iguana in the mud. It had a single puncture wound in its flank, perhaps inflicted by a heron's beak. Blindly it looked at me with one ant-eaten eye.

It turns out that that girl's baby wasn't sleeping, it was dead. Ridley told me, he thought I knew. While we were in Kayun's hut, J.C. and another boy buried the body in the maize patch. Those palm-fibre animals I saw on Kayun's table were to put on the grave. To ward off demons, or keep the spirit from walking, I'm not sure which.

Ridley says Birkenshaw is probably the father. I should have realised: those coppery glints in its hair I noticed in the dugout on my first day. Ridley thought I knew about that too.

I think Ridley tolerates what Birkenshaw gets up to because Birkenshaw keeps quiet about his own predilections. Neither one snitches on the other to the Professor – who doesn't strike me as a man to tolerate perverts on his dig.

As for Ridley's payment to Kayun, maybe that's also to buy his silence? Or maybe he's paying the uncle to get close to the nephew? It's all rather disgusting, and it makes me long to be on my own in the old-growth forest.

I keep thinking about that baby. It wasn't much of a life. Sick for most of it, then stuffed down a hole and eaten by ants. And its mother calmly grinding maize with the body beside her.

Was it because Birkenshaw's the father that she didn't care? Or don't they feel grief as we do? J.C. is her cousin, what does he feel about it? What does Kayun feel about his brother? Mutilated, his blood sprayed over the rocks.

That baby's swaddled remains put me in mind of the lopsided carcase in the museum in Mexico City. I wish I hadn't thought of that.

Ah but the man's a *fake*. He didn't see anyone beside me, *because there was nothing to see.*

Why doesn't that make me feel better? Why this sudden plunge of appalling despair?

Because Kayun was my last hope. Now I have nowhere to hide. I have to face the truth. She's dead. The thread between us has been cut, and it's lashed back with lacerating force. Pain is all I have left.

Eighteen

The past few days have been dismal. Three more ceibas fogged and still no mantids. I've two months left and nothing to show for it.

And always at the back of my mind: What if she *was* in Kayun's hut? Beside me, just as he said?

I can't go on like this. Tomorrow I'm going back to the village to have it out with Kayun.

Next day

I need to write down everything in case I've missed some clue. It felt as if he was playing with me, dropping hints for me to find. Like that *Callimantis* on the roof post – but different.

J.C. didn't ask why I wanted to see his uncle again and we slipped out of camp unnoticed. It was easy. That VIP, Dr Herrera, is back, and Ridley and the Professor are so taken up with him they couldn't care less what I do.

Kayun sat in his hut, puffing on his cigar as if he hadn't moved in a week. If he was taking *muktan*, he gave no sign of it. He regarded me without surprise. He knew I'd be back.

'Is she here now?' I said without preamble.

'Did you call to her?' he said calmly.

'What?'

'Did you summon her?'

'I – yes. But I didn't think it worked. Is she here now?'

'Do you feel her?'

'Don't play with me! *Is she here?*'

'Do you feel her?'

'But how *can* she be? She died thousands of miles away!'

He snorted a laugh. 'You think they need roads?'

It was raining, as it had been all morning. Water was pouring from the eaves, cutting us off from the village, where J.C. sat smoking cigars with the men in their hut.

Did I feel her? No. Did I want to? Yes. No. I don't know. A dead girl. An angry girl. Unseen beside me. Even writing the words makes me go cold.

And yet – what if, when I summoned her at the dig – what if she did come, and I missed my chance to beg her forgiveness? That's what took me back to that grubby little Indian today.

'Why did you agree to see me again?' I asked.

'Because you pay.' He finished counting my money and stowed it in his airline bag.

I was soaked from the river trip and the smell in the hut was making my head ache. Tobacco smoke and whisky, with a pungent undertow of rotting vegetation. No *Callimantis* today. The macaw hunched moodily on its perch. The bottles of Johnnie Walker stood on the table beside the grindstone; both were empty. The orchids were gone from the cross, only the plastic tulips remained.

The macaw flew onto Kayun's shoulder. He took a palm nut from a bowl on the table and held it up and the bird grasped the rock-hard nut in one foot and gave a rattling purr. Putting the nut to its fearsome white beak, it cracked it as easily as if it had been a peanut.

When I was a boy, I loved the mangy old macaw at the zoo. My family found my devotion embarrassing; Edwin said it was cissy. None of them could see what I did: that the macaw had plucked out its feathers because it was sad. Because, like the dead-eyed jaguar pacing its cage, it was missing the jungle. I fantasised about setting them free. The jaguar would be gone in a heartbeat, but the macaw would be grateful, it would become my faithful companion. The bullies at school would gape at the magnificent bird on my shoulder and I would stare them down with freezing contempt. If Edwin so much as looked at me wrongly, I would set my macaw on him and he would flee in terror, humiliated and vanquished for ever.

I almost fancied that Kayun knew all this, that he was flaunting his bond with the bird on purpose. 'Let's stop prevaricating, shall we?' I said crisply. 'I need *muktan*.'

'Why.'

'To contact her. That's what it's for, isn't it?'

'*Muktan* takes you where your spirit wants to go.'

'Don't give me riddles.'

'If your spirit is open to the dead, they come.'

'What does that mean?'

He fed the macaw another palm nut. The bird took it and flew back to its perch.

I said, 'That's why you went to that cave, isn't it? Where

you heard the wind screaming. You went to take *muktan* and find your brother's ghost.'

I'd taken a risk mentioning his brother. The Indian's mahogany features remained impassive, but his dark eyes hardened. 'That place,' he said coldly, 'is not for white men. *Muktan* is not for white men.'

'I'll pay whatever you want.'

He spat, a gobbet landing close to where I sat. 'Yes, white men always pay.' He spoke quietly, with insulting precision. 'They come first when we are boys. They bring sickness. My father, mother, sisters all die. Only me and my brother left.' Tilting back his head, he blew smoke in my face. 'We're too sick to bury them, we have to leave them for the animals to eat. And always more white men. Taking our great trees. Destroying our sacred places. Taking. Always taking.'

'Some of your own people sell the great trees.'

'Because white men trick them. White men are like caterpillars, they eat everything. And when the trees are gone, the forest dies. Then the rivers die and the earth blows away. Only Yachikel left.' He stubbed out his cigar on the floor. 'We are the true people. You white men are a mistake. You're like the wooden men the gods made before they made us. You have no memory, nothing here in your heart.' He struck his chest with his maimed fist. 'You can never get it back.'

'If we're desecrating the dig site, why work there?'

'Because you pay!'

The macaw screeched and stretched its neck, its white eye-patches flushing angry red. '*Xayaxché* is finished,' spat the Indian with a fervour he hadn't shown before. 'White men scrabble like ant-eaters at the sacred stones. We take their money to protect what's left.'

Abruptly the downpour stopped. The heat came surging back. Mosquitoes whined about my head. 'If you want money,' I said, 'here's more. Give me *muktan*.'

The macaw flew out of the hut and vanished into the jungle. The Indian twisted round to watch it go, turning his back on me. 'Get out,' he said over his shoulder. 'Don't come here again.'

Muktan is not for white men.

Well, to hell with that, Kayun – and to hell with you. I don't need you. I'll find the bloody stuff myself.

Nineteen

I need to approach finding *muktan* as I would any other scientific problem. Put aside emotion and proceed logically, step by step. No jumping to conclusions and no distractions. I've pinned a note to my hammock: *Working in lab, plse don't disturb.*

So. What do we know about *muktan*?

One: it's made from '*some flower that grows on trees*'. And note that Ridley said '*on trees*', not '*some tree's flowers*'. Therefore it must be a vine or an epiphyte.

Two: Ridley said once that Kayun takes the stuff at weekends – which stands to reason. Today is Saturday, but when I saw him a few hours ago he didn't appear to be 'high', so he's probably taking it later. *Therefore* he'd either already prepared the stuff, *or* had the makings to hand. *Therefore* you need to think back and visualise the hut. What was different today, compared with last time?

For one thing, he'd put his Lufthansa bag on the table. Did he do that to hide something?

What else? The orchids were gone from the cross, whisky bottles empty. He probably chucked the orchids when they went off; and I wouldn't put it past him to get through two bottles in a week.

Unless – *unless* it's true what Ridley said, and he doesn't drink, and uses the whisky for '*akij*' stuff?

The orchids. Of course, it all fits. The orchids gone, the smell of rotting vegetation, the whisky. *Muktan is prepared by alcohol extraction!* The oldest, simplest method, known the world over.

Steady. *Steady.* Don't get excited. That first time in his hut there were three different orchids on the cross – and yet Ridley said '*flower*', not '*flowers*'. *Therefore* only one of them must be *muktan*.

So the problem becomes: of the three different orchids, which one is *muktan*?

I've re-read my account of my first meeting with Kayun and tried to picture the orchids on the cross.

There was a big frilly white one, the sort you'd buy in a florist's. A smaller one resembling a pale-green daffodil, and a tiny one, hardly a flower, more like orange-red claws. And not forgetting that scent, *so* familiar. What was it?

Thank God I thought to bring a field guide on Mexican flora. It has a decent section on orchids, though apparently there are over fifteen hundred species – of which only a hundred or so are featured in the book. Terrific. How do I narrow it down?

Well, *muktan* grows on trees. Hence I can rule out anything which grows on rocks, the ground, the understorey, savannas, dry plains and swamps. Stick to rainforests. Lowland ones at that; nothing above, say, 3,000 feet.

That's a guess, but if *muktan* grew in the mountains, Ridley would have said.

'That's a guess'. Ha ha ha. Let's face it, Simon, this whole thing is a guess. For all I know, Kayun already had a sufficient supply of *muktan*, and my deductions are entirely false.

And why am I even doing this? Do I really want it to work? The thought of her coming back – as she is now – fills me with dread. But I have to try. I can't stop now.

I am an idiot. The pale-green daffodil is *vanilla*! How could I not recognise the smell?

Muktan can hardly be vanilla, so that leaves the other two, and I've found both of them in the book. The showy white one is a species of cockleshell orchid. The orangey-red one has no common name; in the photograph its grey-green leaves are lobed, like mistletoe, and its tiny claw-flowers are covered in warts.

Which one is it?

J.C. would know at a glance, but if I showed him the photos he'd only clam up. Therefore I have to trick him into revealing the secret – *and he mustn't know that he's given it away*. That's crucial. I can't find the orchid without his help, but he mustn't suspect what I'm looking for.

I've devised a little trap. I shall tell him I've given up fogging for mantids, and instead I'm studying associations between certain insects and plants. To make this convincing I've spent all day drawing up a list of plausible pairings. Some are well known, such as fire ants and acacia. Others are reasonable guesses, e.g. palmetto and bearded palm weevil. I've chosen two likely insects to pair with my two candidate orchids – a stingless bee and an orchid bee – and I've camouflaged my candidates by including a few other orchids. But I've left out vanilla. If I included all three of the orchids on Kayun's cross, J.C. would smell a rat.

I shall grab him tomorrow after lunch. I'll get him to study my photos of insects and plants, and ask if he can help me find them in the jungle. I shall watch his face like a hawk. See how he reacts.

It worked like a charm!

Once he knew there'd be no more of the hated fogging, J.C. became quite friendly again and eager to help; maybe he feels bad about giving me the cold shoulder before. When I showed him the photos of my insects and flowers, he gave each pair a long, thoughtful look – then a confident nod. *Yes, I can find this for you.* He was concentrating so hard that he never noticed how closely I was watching his face.

I knew at once when we came to the *muktan* orchid. It elicited a faint, almost imperceptible widening of his eyes, then a hasty nod. *OK, turn the page.*

I'll never know how I kept my face blank, when inside I was fizzing. That's it. Those warty orange claws. That's *muktan*.

Twenty

I've got it. At least, I've got the orchids. Haven't a clue how to extract the active principle – but be patient, I'll get there.

I'm scratched all over, I've just stripped naked and tweezered out ticks and thorns, swabbed my bites with promethazine, ditto the cut on my calf; yanked on clean clothes, sprayed myself with DEET. I've worked methodically, despite the reckless elation bubbling inside. *You've got it. You've actually got it.*

We set off early, and instead of fogging gear we took ropes and killing jars. Lots of killing jars, more than we could carry at one go. That was vital to my plan: leave some jars in the dugout for J.C. to fetch later, thus giving me a couple of hours to myself in which to gather the orchids. Assuming we found any.

The field guide says the *muktan* orchid grows at an altitude of 1,000-3,000 feet; so do some of my decoy plants. J.C. was at his friendliest as he led me uphill, eagerly seeking the plants and insects on my list. That made me feel a bit guilty. He's only a boy and I've tricked him into revealing the secret of *muktan*. Taking. Always taking.

He found a fallen palmetto, its bark crawling with splendid black weevils. 'The – worms?'

'Larvae,' I said.

'Yes, larvae.' Putting his fingertips to his lips, he mimed eating. 'Very good to eat.'

Dutifully I collected several weevils to occupy my jars, then some fire ants and orchid bees. The bees were beautiful, tiny armoured miracles of iridescent jade, sapphire and bronze; I was glad I hadn't primed my killing jars with poison. (NB: after supper, remember to set them free.)

As we climbed higher, I scanned the trees with binoculars. I prayed that the *muktan* orchid didn't grow too high in the canopy. If it did, my quest was over.

'Quest' is an odd word to use, but that's how it felt. I was braving the enchanted forest to seek the magic bloom that will reunite me with my love. I wonder if she knows.

An hour out from the river, I saw it: fiery specks thirty feet overhead in the moss-hung branches of a mahogany tree.

Somehow I forced myself to turn away and train my binoculars on a nearby copal – which fortunately was bristling with one of my decoy epiphytes. Feigning interest in the copal, I moved to stand beneath it.

'Damn,' I exclaimed. 'We've run out of killing jars. Sorry, J.C., you'll have to go back to the dugout and fetch the rest.'

He didn't want to leave me alone, he said he was responsible for my safety, but I laughed and said I'd been climbing trees since before he was born. At last he agreed to go, although not before giving the copal a thorough inspection for nasties. That gave me another twinge of guilt.

Once he'd gone, I unpacked my rope, took the jar I'd kept hidden in my rucksack and put it in my collecting bag along with my secateurs. I checked that my machete was secure in its sheath, pulled on my canvas gauntlets and my beekeeper's hat, tucking the net inside my shirt and buttoning the collar tight. My breath sounded unpleasantly loud. I didn't like the way the net shrouded my face, restricting my vision.

I've climbed hundreds of trees, but I've never felt such apprehension as I did then. It wasn't the thought of fire ants or snakes, it was a sense of transgression. And a feeling of being watched.

Of course that's common in a forest, particularly the jungle – because one *is* being watched, by all manner of creatures. They can see you, though you can't see them. But I've never felt it so intensely. Or experienced such a powerful sense of wrongness. Almost hostility.

The mahogany's trunk forked above my head: if I stood at full stretch, I could reach the fork and haul myself up. From there the main branches fountained upwards into the broad symmetrical crown, densely foliated with long, glossy, dagger-like leaves. Vines entwined the trunk and dripped from the boughs, which were clogged with epiphytes and moss. The *muktan* orchid grew in clusters on some of the lower branches, like tiny darts of flame.

The tree didn't want to be climbed. Its bark was rough and flaky, scarred by termites. For a moment as I hoisted myself into the fork, I fancied that the bark twisted into a leer. I was so startled I lost my footing and slid down again, cat's claw thorns ripping furrows in my calf.

Grimly I struggled back to the fork – and came face to

face with a bullet ant. Bloody thing was enormous, like something out of *Quatermass*. Next thing I knew it had disappeared. Where had it gone? No time to check my clothes.

As I struggled higher I glimpsed a sinuous flicker of red, yellow and black. My heart jerked. A coral snake was gliding along a branch, inches from my right arm. I scrambled to avoid it and nearly fell, and by the time I'd regained my balance I'd lost sight of the orchids in the foliage. I gave a panicky laugh. Simon you idiot! You can't see the *muktan* for the trees.

I was trying to make light of it. Isn't the hero supposed to face terrifying ordeals? Battle enchanted trees and hostile vines in his quest for the magic flower? But it was such a surreal experience being up there among the leaves, in that green inhuman world in the sky. I felt completely other. I didn't belong.

My senses were on edge, I noticed everything. A cobalt-blue caterpillar inched towards me, raising its crest of purple spikes. When a grasshopper flashed its yellow underwings in warning, I saw that they were speckled with tiny scarlet mites. People think colourful insects are pretty. What they don't understand is that such beauty means poison. Danger. Stay away.

I felt this intensely when I finally reached the *muktan* orchids. The thing didn't seem like a plant, it didn't seem alive. Perhaps that's because its small lobed leaves are the colour of verdigris, they remind me of the vaults in the churchyard where I grew up. The roots were naked, trailing over the branches like pallid worms. And those rust-red, diseased-looking claws.

As I was snipping them off, a shadow of wings slid across me and I ducked, damn near fell out of the tree. I glanced up, but whatever it was had gone. It had been big, though. As big as a vulture. And what struck me as odd was that I had sensed it at all through the dense canopy above my head.

Suffice to say that I was heartily relieved when the deed was done: when I had a jar full of those warty orange claws safe in my collecting bag, and both feet back on solid ground.

Still half an hour before J.C. was due to return. I wished it was sooner. I didn't like being alone. And I couldn't shake off that feeling of transgression. Of being watched.

I have that feeling now, in the lab. It's grown stronger since we returned to camp.

As a distraction I've turned my desk around again, so that it's facing the ceiba's root disc. I disliked having that thing behind my back. It felt threatening. Better to face it. At least I can see what's coming.

Twenty-One

Why does she mean so much to me? Why will I brave snakebites and broken bones for the faintest chance of seeing her again? Why does she still have a grip on my heart?

The purpose of love is to maximise reproductive success. The human infant is helpless at birth, and thus more likely to survive if raised by two parents; therefore the bond between them must be strong – hence the power of love. Love is a physiological and psychological compulsion which obliterates reason. It has to. That's the whole point.

I know this. I've known it since I first read Darwin at the age of fifteen. At the time I found it reassuring. No need to worry, I thought, it's all just biology. It was only when I met Penelope that I learnt that understanding the rationale for a feeling can't protect you from its effects.

Dr Walker once asked if I was a virgin. I didn't answer him, why should I, bloody cheek. In point of fact I'm not, *viz* Jeannette in Grenoble. We worked in the same lab and sort of drifted into it; then three weeks later we drifted amicably apart. After that I wasn't tempted again. I thought sex didn't matter as much as people say. What matters is connection: the meeting of minds, or consciousnesses or spirits, whatever you want to call it. That's what I thought I had with Penelope.

Of course I was attracted to her physically, but it wasn't only that. In fact when I fantasised about sex with her I couldn't make it happen in my mind, she simply lay there. And yet I fantasised endlessly about us working together. I would be teaching her about mantids and she would be listening and being fascinated, helping me in the lab and in the field, coming with me to conferences. But even then I did all the talking. In my fantasies I could never make her reply.

I think now that's because I didn't know what she would have said. In real life I don't remember her saying much, or perhaps I didn't listen. Except once at our second coffee when she mentioned she'd studied History of Art. I couldn't help smiling, it struck me as so typical of girls of her class. I didn't think she'd noticed, but a bit later when I was complaining about how the great artists never painted insects, she said quite sharply, 'Yes they did, what about Dürer's stag beetle?'

Apart from that, though, I can't remember what she said. So it was hardly a meeting of minds. Was it all merely an illusion, driven by biology?

But even if that's true, it doesn't matter. What I felt for her – what I still feel – is ineffable. Beyond explanation. I loved her and I wanted her to love me. I wanted not to be alone.

*

The generator has just stuttered to a halt, plunging camp into darkness. A few anxious minutes later it coughed to life again and the lightbulb above my head flared. From the Mess came a ragged cheer.

I've unlocked the tea chest and checked my jar of *muktan* orchids. I say 'checked', although what did I expect to find? That they'd mutated in the dark, or mysteriously vanished? Each 'flower' – though that seems too benign a word – is no bigger than my little fingernail: a pair of rust-coloured, wart-encrusted claws, half-open, poised to snap. Somehow their smallness only intensifies their potency and menace. Which is fanciful, I know. I must try not to

I saw something moving in the darkness near the ceiba's roots. I know I did. Or rather, I didn't so much *see* it as sense it. The way one senses a presence in one's dreams.

I've made a thorough check with my torch and of course I found nothing. Nothing except an owl moth in the heliconia. Owl moths sleep hanging upside-down by their feet like bats, with their wings folded, displaying the eye-spots which give them their name. That's what I must have glimpsed without being aware of it, the eye-spots. The feeling of being watched came from my unconscious awareness of those 'eyes'.

It must have been that. Although from where I'm sitting, I can't actually see that moth.

And it did feel as if there was something there. I sensed it watching me. And I knew that it wishes me harm.

What if I call the whole thing off? I could do it right now. Empty my jar of orchids in the jungle. Forget about *muktan*. Get back to work on my mantids.

Part of me would love that. It would be such a godawful relief. And yet somehow I don't think I can.

I have the feeling that it's too late.

Twenty-Two

I feel calmer now. It's 5 a.m. and the howlers have just finished their morning roar. The kiskadees are twittering. Bufo is asleep.

I've been up since three. Last night I was overwrought. After checking the ceiba's roots I suddenly felt spent. It was all I could do to find my way to the sleeping quarters, where the others were turning in. For once I was glad of their company, I needed to be among people. I didn't bother undressing, I simply slumped into my hammock and was out like a light the instant I'd zipped up my net.

Five hours later I came abruptly awake. Oh damn and blast it to hell, I'd forgotten to free the insects from the killing jars.

Getting out of that hammock is *such* a rigmarole. Every single time you've got to grope for your torch in the bag and unzip the net, then grab your boots (upended on their stakes) and yank them on – quickly, don't let the mosquitoes in, and don't let your bare feet touch the ground in case of nasties – then zip up the net behind you again. But I had to do it, I had to free those insects. I couldn't bear the thought of the three dozen killing jars in the lab, imprisoning three dozen innocent moths, beetles, grasshoppers, bees, weevils and ants – each one scaling the walls of its glass tomb in a hopeless bid to escape.

It took ages to unscrew the jars and shake them all out. Most of the insects were still alive, and the fire ants were furious. I didn't risk shaking them out, I simply opened their jars and laid them on their sides behind the heliconia – and if Bufo gets a free meal, fine.

Watching the moths and bees zigzag giddily into the dark, I felt oddly at peace. Releasing them felt right. Who knows, it might even propitiate whatever spirits haunt the forest.

After breakfast

There are two questions to be answered. First: How to prepare *muktan*? Second: How do I take it?

Let's start with preparation. After much agonising I've decided that for the extraction process I shall use only the flowers. True, I did see a few leaves on Kayun's cross, but only one or two, and I can't see how they'd matter. Besides, that grey-green colour really does remind me of churchyards. So I shall allow myself an irrational aversion and discard the leaves.

I suppose calling it 'the extraction process' is a bit rich, given what I have in mind. I shall grind the orchids to a pulp between a couple of stones – stones I intend to fetch from the basilisk stream, for luck. Then I'll slosh on the alcohol, a bottle of tequila which I'm pretty sure I can buy from the cooks. After that it's merely a question of allowing the concoction to steep. I dare not boil it; for all I know, *muktan's* active principle might be degraded by heat. I shall simply cover the mixture and lock it in a tea chest.

How long should I leave it to steep? No idea. For all I know, Kayun makes the stuff in batches and steeps them for weeks. Today is Tuesday. I shall leave my concoction till Saturday. Four nights ought to be enough to extract the active principle.

Which is yet more guesswork, but I don't think I can wait any longer. Come what may, I shall take the stuff on Saturday night. That'll give me Sunday to recover. And on Sunday there'll be no question of being needed at the dig.

I shall take the *muktan* here, in the lab. There's room to set up my hammock and I can tell the others that I need to keep an eye on an experiment overnight.

But take it *how*? Drink it? Smear it on my skin? Boil it down, then burn the residue and inhale the smoke?

How?

Kayun believes he's descended from the ancient Maya. Therefore I think we can assume that he takes *muktan* in the same way that his ancestors took their own filthy brews. And I know that they did use drugs derived from plants, because it says so in the book I've borrowed from Birkenshaw.

That book is actually quite useful. Before their blood-letting rites, the ancient Maya used to fast. Which makes sense when you think about it, you'd expect fasting to heighten the drug's effect; I should have thought of that myself. So it's decided. From Thursday night I shall eat nothing. No one will bat an eyelid if I skip a few meals, people here are always coming down with tummy bugs.

But the question remains. How did the Maya actually take their drugs?

Jesus Christ, they were worse than I thought.

'The Maya élite almost certainly took ceremonial enemas by means of a syringe-bag, probably of leather, fitted with a bone tube. This accounts for the tubes found in Classic Period tombs. Presumably, like some tribes of modern-day Maya, the ancient Maya were aware that a drug administered via an enema works more rapidly than one taken by mouth.'

Well, too bad. No enemas for me, thank you very much indeed. If things go wrong I'm not facing Dr Mendoza demanding to know why I'm bleeding from the rectum. So that's settled. I shall swallow the stuff with a shot of tequila and hope for the best.

If things go wrong.

Bloody hell, Simon, what are you doing? What the hell are you *doing?* On the flimsiest chain of evidence, tacked together with conjecture, hunches and several continent-sized gaps in logic, you are planning to ingest some totally unknown plant alkaloid which might very well prove lethal. And all on the strength of the half-understood rites of a gaggle of ancient savages who thought nothing of pushing a stingray barb through their pricks.

For all you know, you've got the wrong orchid. Or maybe *muktan* isn't even a flower, maybe Kayun was onto you from the start, and he put those orchids on the cross as a blind. Maybe *muktan* is actually a fungus or a lichen or a moss. Maybe it doesn't work – except in the whisky-sozzled brain of some mad witch doctor who thinks he can turn himself into a jaguar.

The strange thing is, I don't care. In my mind I keep seeing the image of the hero prince braving every peril to find his lost love. Yes. Hold onto that.

Because the truth is, I can't face living without her. I have to try to reach her, even if it's only for a moment – and whatever the cost.

I've just unzipped my breast pocket and taken out the talisman. It's lying unwrapped on my desk. As I write, my left forefinger is resting on her dark hair entwining the birch twig.

I do not accept – I *will not* accept – that this is all that is left of her in the world. Something more of her must remain.

And if it does – if Kayun spoke the truth and she *was* beside me on the fifth terrace and then again in his hut – *muktan* will help me find her.

Twenty-Three

Muktan Day: Saturday 1st December 1973 – 6.15pm

I'm light-headed with hunger and nervous as hell. Probably wasn't a great idea to polish off what's left of the tequila, but I needed the Dutch courage. Before me on my desk sits the fruit of my labours: an aluminium mug full of cloudy dark-yellow fluid that looks and smells like infected piss. Am I really going to drink that?

First I ought to jot down how I prepared it. OK, I'm hardly going to publish the results, but the scientific method dies hard. Also I need to take all possible care because this is about Penelope. In the same way I used to take inordinate care on the days when I knew I'd be seeing her: clean hair, clean clothes, I even cleaned and re-filled my fountain pen. I needed everything perfect.

Back to *muktan*. After steeping the pulped orchids for four nights in three-quarters of a bottle of tequila, I filtered the sludge through a clean T-shirt, then added the juice of three lemons cadged from the cook-house – my thinking being that citric acid would aid extraction. Then, having changed my mind about heat degradation, I reduced the liquid by half on a borrowed Primus stove.

For the record, I ought to state that my only experience of taking illicit drugs was twenty years ago at Cambridge, to whit:

- Two tabs of 'speed' – resulting in a dreadful night of jangled nerves, and an unshakeable resolve never to try the stuff again; and

- One joint of cannabis – producing nausea, vomiting and the same resolve. (To Jeremy's disgust I threw up into the bath. He'd bought the weed himself, he said it was first-rate, and after my *faux pas* in the bathroom he abandoned all idea of helping me open the Doors of Perception, to our mutual relief).

As for L.S.D.: nope, never. Why would I ingest a chemical that might make me murder someone or jump out of a window?

Jeremy always said that the trick when taking a new drug is to start on a low dose and work your way up; so I intend to do just that. I shall drink one quarter of what's in the mug, then wait an hour and see what happens. After that I shall increase the dose gradually – *if* I need to.

No more putting it off. Here goes.

7 p.m.: Initial sensations: VILE. So bitter I could hardly force it down. Instant burning sensation on lips, tongue, mouth – which now feel acrid and furred.

5 mins later: Lips, tongue, mouth NUMB. I've prodded

and bitten my lips, can't feel a thing. My mouth belongs to someone else.

10 mins post-*muktan*: I'm *cold*. It's a hot night and I'm shivering, teeth chattering, hands & feet icy. Mouth still numb. I'm also remarkably clumsy, nearly sent the mug of *muktan* flying. (Impaired motor skills may be due to tequila; though I don't feel drunk, merely light-headed.)

15 mins post-*muktan*: The oddest sensation that my bones are melting, my skeleton's coming apart. Also much belching and my stomach is bloated, like that Maya death god. Oh Christ what have I done? Should I call for Dr Mendoza?

40 mins post-*muktan*: *Much* better. Shivers, belching, numbness all gone. Bones back to normal and the light-headedness has subsided to a pleasant tequila-induced haze. Forget Dr Mendoza. Besides, by now he'll be drunk.

1 hour: Nothing. Except that bite in the crook of my elbow is swollen and itching worse than ever. I'm still sitting at my desk, waiting for something to happen. A distant rumour of voices from the Mess, people chatting after supper. This isn't working. I could cry.

2 hrs: Still nothing. To hell with starting low, I've just forced down half the remaining *muktan*. Actually more than half, there's only a quarter of an inch left. I've poured it into a specimen bottle and locked it in a tea chest, in case the doctor needs it for analysis if things go wrong.

(Analysis? Out here?) Camp has settled for the night and the jungle's coming alive. Bufo has begun his rhythmic hammering.

2 hrs 45 mins: Still nothing. The lab is awash with faint moonlight. Strange how it changes things. The dim shapes of tables, chairs, tea chests, rucksack have mutated into unfamiliar presences. I can almost sense them silently passing judgement. A minute ago I took out the talisman. 'Penelope?' I whispered. 'Are you there? Was it because of me that you crashed? – Are you all right?'

What a heel I am, that I should ask first about me, and only afterwards if she's OK. My first thought was of myself.

But that's beside the point. What am I doing, asking a dead girl if she's all right? Jesus, Simon, you're losing it.

3 hrs: Still nothing. Except that just now when I conceded defeat and got into my hammock, I was so clumsy it took me ages to zip myself into my shroud and go through the search-and-destroy rigmarole for mosquitoes. I've got this journal with me in case anything happens. I mean, in case Dr Mendoza finds my comatose body and needs to work out what I've done.

Also, to be on the safe side, I've placed the zinc bucket I borrowed from the guards on the ground by the hammock; because Ridley did say that *muktan* made him vomit.

I'm thirsty and my water bottle is to hand, but I'm resisting the urge to have a drink. I don't want to be running to the latrine while under the influence – which I assume I still am. Bufo, shut the fuck up.

<u>10 mins later</u>: Interesting. If I close my eyes I can see my thoughts streaming in multi-coloured strands. They keep snagging together in knots, then smoothing out again, exactly as they used to do when I was a child, on the edge of falling asleep.

That was weird. A purple dragon just shot past. I had my eyes shut and it zoomed into sight from somewhere behind my left shoulder: a cartoon dragon with a spiky tail and big bat-like wings, it went dipping and diving and snorting fire – or rather, it was blowing elaborate curlicues of lilac-coloured smoke. When I opened my eyes, the thing was gone. The moonlit lab was quiet, nothing untoward. Bufo asleep, only the throbbing ring of frogs.

I can make out the dim shapes of the furniture. The heliconia beyond, and behind it the looming shadow of the ceiba's roots. Do I only see that dragon if I shut my eyes?

Yup. And not only one. The second dragon was buttercup-yellow, it went racing after the purple one. Then a tangerine dragon roared past in hot pursuit, spouting lime-green fire. *Dragons?* Is that all my brain can conjure up? Childish, unoriginal, psychedelic dragons straight out of a Disney cartoon?

Faster and faster they go, whizzing round the railway tracks which my brother built for his clockwork trains when he was twelve. If I open my eyes they're gone. Shut my eyes and they're back, hurtling ludicrously around Edwin's miniature landscape of green felt hills and blobby sponge bushes.

God I feel rough. To hell with dragons, I think I'm going to

That was fun. No time to unzip the net, suddenly my stomach was convulsing and I was retching, sour yellow vomit burning throat and nose, spattering the hammock. For Christ's sake, where did it come from? My stomach's empty, I haven't eaten since Thursday night. It went on for ages. Nothing I could do except pray for the heaving to stop.

When at last it did, I unzipped the net and dragged in the bucket. I'm scribbling this lying in a vomit-soaked foetal curl with the bucket between my journal and my knees. Please, nausea, don't come back.

But I know that you will.

1.10 a.m., 6 hrs post-*muktan*: I want to die. Waves of awfulness, rising to an unbearable peak – then the gut-wrenching release of throwing up. A brief shaky respite, then it starts all over again. And those fucking dragons. So childish. And always *there*, whenever I shut my eyes.

3 a.m.: The dragons are gone. I wish the nausea was too. I've been sick again & again. I've tried sipping water to wash out my stomach but it only makes the retching worse. I'm resigned to my fate. Don't care if I die. Too ill to care.

Twenty-Four

<u>4.10 a.m.</u>: Weirdest experience yet. I hadn't felt nauseous for almost forty minutes and was savouring the blessed relief when I became aware that it was 1938 and I was seven. At the same time I was also the man I am now, who has lost Penelope. I was observing myself in astonishment, because somehow my thoughts and feelings were those of my seven-year-old self. I felt *everything*. My gnawing anxiety about the school bullies, my tearful fury at Edwin for burning the wasps' nest. My guilt because he only learnt of its existence when I took to visiting the shed.

That's where I was, in the shed. I caught its smell of creosote and fermenting grass cuttings, the faint bitter undertow of ash. I'm consoling myself with threepence worth of liquorice and my favourite fairy tale, *The Grateful Animals*. A prince sets off on a journey, during which he saves the lives of a raven, a fish and a wasp. It then transpires that each creature is in fact the king of the ravens, the fishes, the wasps – so that when the prince later finds himself in deadly peril, the grateful animals summon their subjects and come to his aid.

My seven-year-old self adores this tale. I love the fact

that helping animals is rewarded, and an insect plays a vital rôle. Unbeknown to my family, I *am* the King of the Wasps. Soon I will summon my loyal subjects and we will inflict a dreadful punishment on the evil Edwin, destroyer of nests.

I suppose all this was a sort of temporal hallucination, but what was remarkable was its reality. It was vastly more vivid than memory, it had *precisely* the same flavour as when I was a child. Can it be that every nuance of my boyhood still exists in the recesses of my brain?

4.30 a.m.: Never thought I'd be grateful to the howlers for waking me up, but I am. That was horrible.

The first part wasn't. The boyhood stuff had faded, and this time I was lying serenely in my hammock, watching myself transforming into a mantis. I wasn't frightened, I was fascinated. This was what I've always wanted, to become one of them: to experience their world.

As with the previous hallucinations it felt extraordinarily real, although this was vividly tactile. I could *feel* my skin hardening into an exoskeleton, my forearms thinning to brittle sticks, my fingers fusing to form a single vicious hooked claw. Then in a split second everything changed. I found myself drawing my hooked claw across my own throat, slicing through the gristly cartilage of my Adam's apple, my blood jetting with appalling force...

Thank God for those howlers. I don't know what would have happened if I hadn't woken up.

It's getting light. The nausea hasn't returned. I suppose that's something. The last lingering trace of *muktan* is a faint, sulphurous shimmer bathing the lab. And the memory of that final horror – which I shall do my best to forget.

I was wrong about the nausea. I've had one last bout of vomiting, but this time Ridley came and held the bucket under my head. He was surprisingly decent about it, muttering 'Poor old chap.' Then: 'Jesus, what have you done to your hand?'

Apparently during the night I sliced open my palm on the bucket's metal rim. I wasn't aware of it, but there's blood all over the place and my hammock's even more of a mess than I thought. Ridley was aghast. 'You're going to need stitches. Didn't you feel *anything*?'

I said no, and he gave me an odd look; maybe it crossed his mind that I'd tried *muktan*. Then he caught sight of the empty tequila bottle under the desk and broke into his knowing grin. 'Oh dear oh dear, no wonder you're feeling rough. Should've come to Uncle Ridley, I'd have got you the good stuff!'

Perhaps out of long familiarity with hangovers, he did a good job of cleaning me up. Dumped my soiled clothes and bedding in a bucket of river water, swabbed the worst of the mess off the hammock, even found me a fresh pillow because I'm too weak to sit on a chair. He's gone now and I'm lying in comparative comfort, although the cut on my hand is making up for lost time and throbbing viciously.

Dr Mendoza has been and gone. He's given me a tetanus shot and stitched and bandaged my cut (it's my left hand, so I can still write). After checking me over he's ruled out malaria, cholera, Chagas' disease, leptospirosis and haemorrhagic fever. When he saw the tequila bottle he gave a resigned shrug. He's satisfied I've only got a hangover and a touch of fever. Told me to rest and drink plenty of fluids.

I'm no expert on hangovers but I've never had one this bad, my head feels as if it's about to explode. That's probably because, despite Ridley's best efforts, the lab stinks overpoweringly of sick.

A hummingbird is darting about like crazy in the heliconia, I can see its wings going hell for leather, which is doing nothing for my head. To make matters worse, that bucket of filthy linen is black with flies and the buzzing is drilling through my skull.

Actually that buzzing is unnaturally loud. And how come I can even *see* the hummingbird's wings? Why aren't they a blur? Is it possible that *muktan* has in some way sharpened my senses?

Maybe, but that's beside the point. It's time I faced facts. So *what* if *muktan* has heightened my senses? So *what* if it's reduced my sensitivity to pain? The truth is, that is the sum total of its effects. It does bugger all when it comes to contacting the dead.

Well, Simon, what did you expect? A celestial choir and Penelope floating down on a fluffy pink cloud to absolve you of your sins?

Maybe the stuff doesn't work on white men. Maybe you need to be an *akij*, like Kayun. Doesn't matter why. Point is, I went through all that misery for nothing.

Muktan doesn't work.

Twenty-Five

Everyone's being kind to me, it's making me feel worse. They think I'm depressed because of a hangover and I can't tell them the reason for this black despair. She's gone and she's never coming back. I will never know if I killed her. I can never tell her how sorry I am. Never beg her to forgive me.

She is gone. And I will be forever alone.

From where I lie, I can see the tea chest in which I locked the remains of the *muktan*. I can feel it mocking me. When I'm stronger I shall empty the specimen bottle in the jungle. I never want to see the filthy stuff again.

Thinking back over the past week, I don't recognise myself. All those 'logical' deductions which had nothing to do with logic. That despicable trick to make J.C. betray the secret of *muktan*. My reckless assault on the mahogany tree. My infantile glee in concocting that ridiculous potion. I am appalled by my capacity for unreason. My pathetic eagerness to ignore the truth.

And all for nothing. Beneath the shame and the self-loathing, a yawning emptiness. Ever since I came to Mexico I've been clutching at straws. Well, a birch twig. I can no longer do that, because now I know it's over. I've failed. Nothing left to try.

Well that was a turn-up for the books. The Professor just came to see me and he was *nice*. It's made me feel a bit better.

He stood uncertainly under the eaves of the lab, as if waiting for me to ask him in. Gruffly he enquired how I felt, and when I said pretty grim, he said, Ah well, it happens to everyone. We looked at each other, then away. I wondered if, like me, he was remembering the little *contretemps* I'd witnessed between him and Ridley when I'd happened across them in the Mess. I had bought the tequila and was leaving the cook-house when I heard voices. The Professor and Ridley were standing practically nose-to-nose, hissing and spitting at each other under their breath. I didn't catch what was said, and when they saw me they broke off and glared at me till I left.

Now I watched the Professor draw up a chair and sit. He cleared a space on my desk for the canvas bag he'd brought. 'Survival pack,' he said. 'Eat nothing for the next twelve hours.'

I gave a hollow laugh. 'My stomach quails at the mere notion of food.'

He opened his mouth to reply, then shut it again. Ran his thumbnail over the grain of the desk.

Again I wondered what that row with Ridley had been about. Had the Professor just learnt of his right-hand man's predilections? Or had I got it all wrong, was what I saw in the Mess a lovers' tiff?

The thought was so bizarre that I almost laughed. I

covered it up by asking how things were going at the dig.

'What d'you mean?' the Professor said sharply.

'I don't know. Any good finds?'

He shook his head.

I asked if the 'Temple' really was a temple. This seemed to be safer ground and he became quite animated, said he's convinced that it is. I asked if he's found a temple before and he said no, but once he found a tomb. 'In fact I nearly made the discovery of a lifetime.' To my surprise, his rugged features became wistful. 'Few years ago, not far from here. I knew it was a tomb because I stuck in a wire and it came out with traces of cinnabar. They used to smear that on bones.' He shot me a glance, as if to check that I wasn't bored.

'Couldn't believe my luck,' he went on. 'Thought I'd found the next Palenque. And d'you know, for a moment when we opened it up, the beam of my torch caught *an entire bolt of cloth*?' He frowned, moved the bag on the desk a fraction to the right. 'You've no idea how rare that is. In the jungle, everything rots. We have no Maya textiles, can only guess how they wrapped their dead. And yet there it was, that cloth.' Again he shook his head. 'Of course, the next moment the whole thing crumbled to dust.' He cleared his throat. 'Worst moment of my life.'

I mumbled that I was sorry, and his mouth twisted in a weary smile. 'Oh, everyone has some story about a near-miss in the jungle. The lost shrine they stumbled across, then couldn't find again. That sort of thing.'

I made to reply, but he said briskly, 'Right, let's get you better.' Flipping open the bag, he took out a red vacuum flask and put it on the desk. 'Sip what's in this every now and then.' I asked what the flask contained and he said boiled water, sugar and salt. 'Tastes awful, but trust me it works. And tonight – *if* you're up to it – drink this.' He set a green flask beside the red one. 'Sweet tea. Dry crackers in the tin, have a few if you're hungry. And if you spot blood in your stools, call Mendoza *at once*.' He slapped his knees and stood up. 'Best thing you can do is nothing. Let your body recover. See you tomorrow.'

I would have preferred his usual bombast. Sympathy had brought me absurdly close to tears.

It's dark and I've been watching the moths circling the lightbulb above the hammock. There's a theory about why they do that. It's thought they use the moon as a fixed marker to find their way, and that they mistake a night-light for the moon. This is what dooms them. By keeping the light at a constant angle, the unlucky moth ends up spiralling inwards to its death.

A tiger moth has just fallen lifeless onto my mosquito net. With my preternatural eyesight I can make out every one of the jewelled scales on its wings: sapphire, ruby, nacreous white. If I didn't owe my enhanced vision to *muktan*, I'd be delighted. As it is, I want my imperfect human senses back. This is putting me on edge. I don't know what I'm going to see next.

The following day, afternoon

Still ridiculously weak, and time hangs heavy. I wanted Dr Mendoza to give me a sleeping pill, but Birkenshaw tells me he's having a liquid lunch and not to be disturbed. Apparently that's what did for his practice in Chiapas: too many liquid lunches.

I haven't the energy to move back to the communal sleeping quarters – though I am in slightly better spirits, probably because this morning I managed to keep down some boiled rice. I even staggered to the latrine by myself. (The guards nodded at me through their cigar smoke – which still smells preternaturally vile – and went on chatting.)

An hour ago I lugged the bucket containing my soiled linen down to the river. I had to pause every so often and wait for my knees to stop trembling. After giving the shallows a cursory check for caimans, I slopped my clothes and bedding around for a bit. Didn't have the strength to wring them out properly, simply bundled them back into the bucket and hauled it back to the lab. It took all my remaining strength to string up a line and hang up the sodden things, and by the time I'd finished, black spots were zooming before my eyes. I barely had the will to slump into my hammock and zip the net. Couldn't face despatching the mosquito whining in my ear.

It's 2.48 in the afternoon and camp is deserted, everyone's up at the dig. A moment ago a blue and green parakeet alighted in the heliconia. Its screeches are piercing my temples like hot wire. I've told it to bugger off, but it goes on screeching.

The generator is deafening and its petrol reek is making me queasy – though luckily not nauseous. The clothes line is the worst, the water pattering onto the palm fronds on the floor sounds like a regular downpour.

I'm bored. I want to go to sleep and not wake up till I'm better, and every last trace of *muktan* is out of my system.

The guards have gone back to their posts, shaking their heads in bemusement, and Dr Mendoza has given me a pill to calm me down. He says it'll chase away what he calls my 'fever dream'. As he was leaving he gave me an odd look, as if he suspects that I haven't told him everything. Too right I haven't.

And I haven't taken his pill. I need to make sense of what just happened. But one thing's for sure. What I experienced was no dream.

As soon as I woke up I knew something was wrong. The air had turned heavy and oppressive. I took deep breaths, but still felt breathless. I looked at my watch: 3.14 p.m. I'd only been asleep a few minutes – and yet everything had changed. Every muscle in my body was tense. My good hand was clenched in a fist, and I was holding my injured one rigid, it was hurting like hell. That's how I knew I was awake. That and the crawling sensation on my forearms, the back of my neck, my scalp. Every hair on my skin was standing on end. I thought: it is mid-afternoon. Broad daylight. I am awake. I am afraid.

Then all at once a violent gust of wind was blowing in from the jungle, rushing over the ceiba's root disc and through the heliconia, sweeping the papers off my desk, knocking over the Professor's flasks. I could see the para-keet flapping its wings to keep its balance. It was screeching, but no sound came. I could see the heliconia thrashing, the papers scattering, the water raining from my wet clothes onto the floor – but I couldn't hear any of it, not even my own panting breath or my hammering heart. I was caught in that thick, oppressive, unnatural silence.

A powerful urge came over me to turn my head and look behind me. I intensely did *not* want to do this, I dreaded what I might see – and yet the urge was overwhelming.

I turned my head.

She was standing beside the hammock. Indistinct, yet horribly real – and very, very dead. Behind the floating darkness of her hair her face was a shifting, particulate shadow, like whirling dust motes, I couldn't make out her features. But I saw her hands. Her fingers gripped the edge of the hammock and they were bony and fleshless, the grey skin mottled. Her long sharp fingernails penetrated the mosquito net as if it didn't exist. It flashed across my mind to wonder how this could be. Then she was leaning over me with appalling intent and I was trapped with her in that terrible silence. I felt her ill will, her malevolence. Now she was bending closer, and her head was passing right through the net, as if it were smoke—

I screamed. I went on screaming, clawing at the zip, tumbling out of the hammock onto the ground.

The guards ran up. Moaning, I clutched at their legs.

The parakeet flew off with a squawk. From the wet clothes on the line, water pattered onto the floor.

Twenty-Six

Night

What if it really was her? What if she did come to my call?
Dead. Angry. Bent on revenge.

I can't believe I'm writing this. It's not rational, I know
she wasn't real. And yet some deep part of myself can't
leave it alone. My thoughts spiral endlessly inwards. It's
like picking at a scab.

In fairy tales visitations come in threes. Three times she
has come to me. Once at the dig site, then in Kayun's hut,
and now by my hammock.

Will she come again?

The following day

Extraordinary how different I feel after ten hours' sleep.
Last night I moved my hammock back to the communal
sleeping quarters. No more bunking alone in the lab, thank
you very much. Best thing I ever did. I no longer mind
Ridley's smoker's cough or Watts' frequent visits to the

latrine, Birkenshaw's stuttering snores. They're human and reassuring. They keep the jungle at bay.

Of *course* what I saw wasn't real, it was a waking dream. And I definitely was awake. I could feel the pain in my hand, I could see the water from my wet clothes hitting the ground – even if I couldn't hear it. That's the clue, the silence. What I experienced *felt* real but it wasn't, it was *muktan*. Delayed effect.

I know this because my perceptions remain heightened, which means the stuff is still in my system. Hence the inescapable conclusion: what I saw was an hallucination. Intensely vivid, but hallucination nonetheless. Like the kind you experience when you're falling asleep. There's a name for it, hypna-something-or-other.

And come to think of it, it's hardly surprising if my mind was playing tricks. For months I've been obsessing about Penelope, then I go and take a mind-altering drug. What did I expect?

But why was she so horrifying? So – malevolent, even?

Well, because she's dead. And because, rightly or wrongly, I blame myself. And because of the bloody Mayas' fixation on violent death, which poisons the whole atmosphere of the dig.

And because of Kayun's little mind-games. Let's not forget those.

Next day

My senses remain preternaturally sharp, even when it comes to people. I discovered that this morning when I climbed to the top terrace to see the Professor.

I found him working alone and when I greeted him he nearly jumped out of his skin. 'Christ, man!' he exclaimed. 'Are you trying to give me a heart attack?'

I apologised, and said I wanted to volunteer my services. He seemed surprised. Made some remark about the prodigal son, and maybe he could find something for me to do on the lower terraces. He'd swiftly recovered his usual bombast, and as we made our way down, he gave me a little lecture on how the site would have appeared a thousand years ago. 'Of course all the carvings would've been picked out in brilliant colours – red, blue, yellow, green – plazas and facings in dazzling white. Must've been astonishing.' He flushed, perhaps embarrassed at being caught using his imagination.

To show willing I remarked that producing so much lime would have needed tons of firewood, and he beamed as if I'd said something profound. Turns out he has some pet theory that this is what scuppered the Maya: they simply cut down too many trees. 'None of that rubbish about internecine wars,' he scoffed. 'They destroyed the forest, that's what did for them.' He was talking too much even for him, and I had the curious impression that he was trying to distract me; although from what, I had no idea.

And it wasn't only from him that I kept sensing things. We passed Marshall and Watts working with their trowels near a party of Indians hefting rocks, and I received flashes of what they were thinking. The archaeologists were losing faith in the dig, the Indians wondering how long it would last and whether they'd get paid. On the terrace below, Ridley was worrying that Kayun might demand more money, while Birkenshaw felt demeaned by his pursuit of children, yet couldn't bring himself to stop.

It was similar to telepathy, and deeply unsettling – although of course it was merely impressions, I wasn't really picking up their thoughts, I couldn't be. But I don't like it, and I wish it would stop.

How long does *muktan* stay in the system? If I asked Kayun, would he tell me the truth?

Six days post-*muktan*

The Professor never did find me anything to do, and I've been free to go my own way. I've had an excellent day's work upriver, and despite the odd unpleasant moment I've been completely absorbed. No more telepathy – and no more fogging. I've searched for mantids the old-fashioned way, by eye, and although I haven't found any, I have come across several fascinating egg-cases. One is long and narrow, reminiscent of the African mantids such as *Trachodula*; another – attached to a fallen ceiba leaf – resembles a tiny narrow-necked flask. Of course I can't assume they're new species, but it's a promising sign.

As for my heightened perceptions, I've decided to enjoy them. It was such fun wrong-footing J.C. in the jungle today! He couldn't understand why I kept spotting things before he did, and he looked so bemused that I almost laughed aloud.

As we were making our way through the understorey, I led us unerringly to a tree boa's decomposing carcase beneath a mahogany. To my delight I found that I could actually hear the carrion beetles' minute crunchings and suckings. I even caught the chlorophyll scent from a line of leaf-cutters wobbling along the tree's roots; and when I put my hand on its trunk I sensed its whole history through my palm, from seed to sapling to leafy giant.

That's when it happened. By chance I was gazing down at my hand on the trunk when something shifted in my perceptions, and for a moment the back of my hand turned scaly and supple as a snake's. It was only a fleeting impression, yet arresting enough to make me sway on my feet – because for that one instant I felt myself *becoming* snake. Then normality returned, and I knew that what I was looking at was merely the play of leaf-shadow on the network of veins beneath my skin.

Thinking of it now, it puts me in mind of something I read in Birkenshaw's book. There's a theory that the ancient Maya created their complicated images nesting within each other because they perceived no boundary between animal and human – between the living and the dead. It's a disorientating idea which reminds me unpleasantly of Kayun. And if it were true, it would mean the spirits are ever-present. They're among us all the time. Even inside us.

But as I said, it was only the impression of a moment. And J.C. had noticed nothing: as usual he was forging ahead, hacking at the undergrowth with his machete. I hurried to catch up.

I hadn't gone far when I caught a low, steady buzzing from somewhere beyond him. 'J.C.!' I called in a hoarse whisper. 'Come back! Wasps' nest!'

The boy halted to listen. Shook his head, gave me a questioning look. 'I can't hear anything.'

'Sh!' I put my finger to my lips.

Sure enough, a wasp lit onto my sleeve. She was a paper wasp, genus *Polybia*, not sure which species, but bound to be aggressive, most paper wasps are. Delicately she investigated my sweat-soaked shirt, while I admired her elegant striped thorax, her translucent wings which could beat faster than a nerve impulse can travel to my brain.

Her sister flew in, her long legs dangling, and landed on my breast pocket. Then another. For a moment all three raised their tiny heads and met my gaze (at least, that's how it felt). I stayed very still and kept my breathing shallow, so as not to alarm them. They were scouts. If they perceived a threat to the nest, they would summon reinforcements and attack.

But I wasn't scared, I was moved. Everything flooded back: the wasps' nest in the shed when I was a boy. My eyes stung as I gazed down at the beautiful little creatures on my shirt. *I'm sorry,* I told them silently. *Sorry I couldn't stop Edwin finding the nest. Sorry I couldn't save you.*

J.C. had seen none of this, he was continuing up the path.

Two more wasps flew onto my shirt, then another three. Slowly, so as not to aggravate them, I went after the boy. 'J.C.!' I hissed.

He spun round.

I pointed past him. 'That nest sounds big! Can you really not hear it?'

Again he shook his head; but ever-protective, he motioned me to stay put and started forwards, placing his bare feet with noiseless care. He'd gone about thirty feet when he gently lifted a branch with his stick – and there was the nest, the size of a football, beautifully constructed of chewed wood and wasp spit, and speckled with tiny dark bodies. As yet they were reasonably calm. The next stage would be a black flood of wasps emerging to cover the whole nest. After that the swarm would attack.

J.C. was gaping at me.

Forcing a grin, I jerked my head in the direction of the river. *Let's get out of here!* I mouthed.

As we were paddling back to camp, he twisted round and said, 'That nest. How come you heard it so soon?'

I chuckled. 'Must be getting my eye in. Or should I say my ear?'

And yet it does strike me as peculiar that those wasps should have flown straight past J.C. and alighted on me. And they looked at me, only at me.

Although when you think about it, what's strange about that? No doubt they were attracted to me rather than J.C. because sweat-soaked cotton smells more strongly than rain-washed skin. And they eyeballed me because *I* was looking at *them*.

In that way, animals are like people. They know when they're being watched.

Twenty-Seven

It wasn't her. It was never her. I've been wrong, wrong, wrong.

It had been pelting since mid-morning, and around eleven the Professor had called a halt to the dig and everyone had piled into the Mess.

A holiday mood, rain pounding on the roof and streaming off the eaves, shutting us in for an afternoon's drinking. Ridley had rapped out his punchline and our table had erupted with laughter. At the other end of the Mess, the Indians grinned and raised beer bottles in salute.

We Europeans had been setting the world to rights. By now every man knew his role in the group. The Professor was the worldly yet committed leader, adept at *realpolitik*; Birkenshaw the Bertie Wooster buffoon, Ridley our friendly neighbourhood drop-out, Marshall and Watts the chorus – and I was the dry-as-dust scientist who refused to be impressed by the Maya.

'I just don't see the appeal,' I insisted, to universal groans. 'Torture? Mutilation? What's so great about that?'

Replies came thick and fast: 'Astronomy?' 'Maths?' 'Architecture!' 'Books!'

'And lashings of blood,' I put in. 'No wonder the poor sods took to Christianity: instead of being sacrificed, they got wine every Sunday.'

More groans, and I rose to fetch coffee for Marshall and me (he doesn't drink, and I've been off alcohol since *muktan*). I was in a good mood. All right, my senses aren't completely back to normal but the telepathy has gone and I was enjoying being with people.

I was returning with the coffee when it happened. I was edging between the Indians' tables, clutching a brimming mug in either fist when I caught sight of Kayun sitting at the table on my left. I couldn't see his face as another Indian was in the way, but I knew it was Kayun because I recognised his build and his scrawny forearms; so on impulse I decided to ask him how long the effects of *muktan* last. No harm in trying. He might even tell me the truth.

'Kayun!' I called, raising my voice above the din.

He didn't respond, so I shouted again. *'Akij!'*

Marshall was waving at me, shouting something about coffee, and at the same moment I spotted Kayun – I mean, the real Kayun. He was sitting at the *other* table, the one to my right; crouching with his muddy feet drawn up on the bench, his T-shirt tented over his knees, watching me intently.

'Hey, Corbett!' Marshall called. 'While you're at it we could do with more—'

I didn't hear the rest. A wall of silence had slammed down between me and the world. The clamour of voices, Marshall shouting – all had sucked back like a wave, leaving me trapped. The air was heavy and thick in my throat, I laboured to breathe. I tried to move, but my feet were rooted to the ground. As if through water I was dimly aware of life going on around me – cooks ladling rice and beans, men laughing and smoking, tilting back their chairs, sucking beer bottles – but I couldn't hear any of it. Existence had ripped apart and from out of the darkness had come – what?

I was still facing Kayun, but I knew – I *knew* – that I had to turn and confront what I'd mistaken for him: what sat at the head of the table behind me.

It wasn't moving and yet it was ever-changing, a shadow breaking and re-forming like a swarm. But I did see it. I saw its scrawny forearms, the skin mottled and stretched. I saw its long dark floating hair. Something was horribly wrong with its throat: a ruin of torn flesh, a dark flood seeping. And from its faceless void I felt its menace. Its still dead core bent on me.

I tried to cry out but my tongue stuck to the roof of my mouth. The thing's malevolence fixed me like a beam.

Next moment I dropped the mugs and the din of the Mess came roaring back. '–sugar!' Marshall was shouting. 'Hey, Corbett! You forgot the sugar!'

Blankly I stared at him. I turned back to the Indians' table. The thing was gone.

On the other table Kayun crouched on his bench, his T-shirt tented over his knees. Watching me.

He knew what I'd seen. He *knew*.

The Indians were leaving, Kayun among them. I ran after him and tripped, fell headlong between the tables.

By the time I got outside he was halfway to the river. Rain was still pelting down, the walkway was ankle deep. Within moments I was soaked.

Thrusting aside the others, I grabbed Kayun's shoulder and yanked him round. 'Why is it after me?' I yelled. 'What is it? What does it want?'

He was slight as a boy, barely reached my breastbone, but his dark gaze repudiated mine. Behind him stood the other Indians, a wall of mute resistance.

My hand dropped to my side and I took a step back. 'Make it leave me alone,' I panted.

'Go back to your country, *ts'ul*,' he said above the clatter of rain on leaves. 'You shouldn't be here.'

'Make it stop! I haven't *done* anything!'

He spoke to me again, something brief and cold in Yachikel. Then, slowly and with finality, he slid one palm over the other, brushing off his hands. And walked past me down to the river.

That time when I was on the fifth terrace and I tried to summon Penelope. Something came. But it wasn't her. It was never her.

As I write this the lab looks altered. Tables, chairs, tea chests, my rucksack, all the familiar, inanimate objects – they've turned against me. *You're on your own. What are you going to do?*

After I'd taken *muktan* and that thing bent over me in the hammock, I felt its malevolence. I felt it again just now in the Mess. Directed at me.

'*Muktan* draws the dead,' Kayun said once. 'The dead',

that's what he said. Not 'her'. But I heard what I wanted to hear. I told myself that it had to be her.

For the record, I'm not mad. My breakdown was depression, not psychosis. Dr Walker's pills were only diazepam to help me sleep and I took them sparingly, didn't want to get addicted. I haven't taken one since I left London.

I've thought of something else. The other day when it leant over my hammock, it vanished the moment the guards ran in. But this time in the Mess I was among people when it appeared, and they were no help. I was cut off. Alone with it in that terrible silence.

What is it?

Is it getting stronger?

What does it want?

Twenty-Eight

Later

The worst thing is the isolation. The feeling of being hunted. Cut off from the herd.

I'm writing this in the lab. The others are still in the Mess. But even if I went back and blurted it all out, they wouldn't believe me. I'd still be on my own.

I am a white man and what I saw in the Mess was Indian. Therefore it has reason to hate me. That much I know. But what does it *want*? Is it after revenge because I fogged the ceibas? And why do I have this sense that I've been led here? That I was *meant* to break their taboo by fogging those trees. That I was *meant* to take *muktan*.

One thing's for sure. The only man who can help me is Kayun. He knows what I saw. I have to get him to make it stop. Only he can do that.

Next day

Kayun hasn't been seen in camp, or at the dig. I can't find J.C.

to take me to the village and no one else will go with me; and I can't go alone because the Professor has vetoed solo dugout trips, he says the river is too high and too fast, too much débris. He's even posted a guard on the bank to make sure that no one tries. So I'm stuck. Waiting for it to come again.

Midnight

All my life I've believed that knowledge gives you power. That there's no sense remaining in the dark, if you have a problem you need to find out as much as you can about what you're up against. I don't believe that any more. Sometimes it's better not to know.

36 hours since it happened. And though I've thought of it constantly, I realise now that I've been in denial. Well, not any more. Why did I mistake that thing in the Mess for Kayun? It wasn't purely because it was scrawny and Indian, there was more to it than that. I recognised its forearms because of the black bands tattooed on its wrists: the mark of the *akij*.

This evening I tackled Ridley. The others were still in the Mess and we were alone in the sleeping quarters, getting ready to turn in. Ridley was drunk but functioning, shaking out his bedding. I was pretending to fiddle with my hammock's fastenings, while darting glances at the dripping darkness beyond the hut. If that thing can appear in the Mess, it can appear anywhere.

'Kayun's brother,' I said. 'How did he die?'

Ridley peered at me blearily. 'What? Why on earth bring that up now?'

'I don't know, I just wondered. What happened to him?'

Without unbuttoning his shirt he yanked it over his head, bundled it into a ball and unzipped his mosquito net long enough to stuff it inside as a pillow, while transferring his cigarette from hand to hand with the practised motions of the chain-smoker. 'I thought I told you. We don't know.'

'You know more than me.'

'Not much. He'd been dead for days by the time we found him. Pretty messed up by scavengers.'

I opened the pouch at the head of my hammock and stared at its contents. I drew the drawstring shut. 'What did they do with the – remains?'

'I don't know. The Indians saw to it.'

'But surely you—'

'Corbett, it's not something you ask. Even if I had they wouldn't have told me. Some things they never tell an outsider.'

'Could it have been an animal attack? Jaguar? Caiman?'

He took a drag on his cigarette and exhaled, narrowing his eyes against the smoke. 'I told you before. No animal would have done that.'

'Done what?'

He ground his cigarette under his boot and lit another. When I realised he didn't intend to answer, I tried again. 'You said once that there was blood sprayed on the rocks.'

'So I did,' he replied with an edge to his voice. 'Mendoza reckons his throat was cut. Among other things.'

His throat was cut. My mind flashed to the vision I'd experienced on *muktan*. Clawing my throat, slicing across my Adam's apple. Coincidence. It had to be. Or maybe I'd heard something about Kayun's brother, then forgotten it until *muktan* dredged it up from my unconscious.

Ridley was regarding me oddly, and I saw that I was gripping my hammock with both hands. 'So he was murdered,' I said.

'That's what people say. Prof thinks it was loggers, or maybe cattlemen.'

'What about you? What do you think?'

He shook his head. 'Too messy. Not their style.'

'Could it have been other Indians?'

'Nah. The man was an *akij*, they'd never dare.'

'So what d'you think happened?'

He inhaled deeply, blew out a thin stream of smoke. 'I've always thought he might have done it himself.'

'*What?* Cut his own throat?'

'It's been known to happen.'

'But why? Was he depressed?'

'That's not what I mean.'

'He'd have to be depressed to commit suicide.'

'I told you, that's not what I mean.'

I waited.

He hesitated. 'You know, Corbett, I've lived with these people for twenty years and I've still no idea how they think.' Again he exhaled. He watched the smoke snaking into the rafters. 'He wasn't depressed, he was angry. He hated what we were doing. A few weeks before he died he stopped working on the dig. Used to hang around shouting, berating us. Rattled the hell out of the other Indians, I tried everything to make him stop. It was a relief when one day he didn't turn up.' He paused. 'If you really want to know, I think he wanted a violent death so he could be with the gods. Maybe he thought it'd make him stronger. Better able to fight us.'

'You think he slit his own throat to make himself stronger?'

'I told you, they're not like us. You can't expect consistency, everything neatly tidied away. But yes, I think maybe something mattered to him more than his own life. And no, I haven't a clue what that 'something' might have been.'

I pictured blood spattered on rocks. I thought of the picture in that woman's book on the plane. The little scarlet snakes jetting from the priest's erect penis.

Suddenly I was furious. 'Jesus *Christ*,' I burst out. 'Why are these people obsessed with blood? Why can't they get it through their heads, it's just a fluid! It carries oxygen and nutrients and that's *it*! Nothing sacred, no magic power to wash away sins! You'd think they'd know by now!'

Ridley laughed. 'Try telling them that. Anyway, what's all this to you?'

What could I tell him? *I'm angry because I'm frightened. Because it's after me.*

What's after you, Corbett? The ghost of a dead Indian shaman? And why?

I don't know. I don't know. I don't know.

Later

Earlier in the day I learnt from Ridley that Kayun isn't in the village, he's gone into the jungle to do *akij* things. I waylaid J.C. at lunch but he was as slippery as an eel, said he'd no idea where his uncle has gone.

I caught the boy again as he was leaving for the village in his dugout. He was friendly enough, though he didn't want to talk to me in front of the other Indians, so I've hired him to go upriver tomorrow, I told him I have work to do in the old-growth forest. Once we're alone in the jungle he'll have to tell me. He is Kayun's nephew, he must know where he is.

I suppose what I saw in the Mess might have been some kind of unconscious suggestion, or perhaps telepathy, emanating from Kayun himself. In a way that would make sense. A lot more sense than jumping to the conclusion that it was the ghost of his murdered brother. It would simply mean that I had a waking nightmare of a dead Indian – which, when you think about it, is entirely to be expected. A savage, unexplained killing would prey on anyone's mind.

I write all this because as a scientist I'm trained to consider every possible explanation, but I don't believe it for a moment. I know it's not true. What I saw in the Mess was not my mind playing tricks and it was not telepathy or unconscious suggestion. It was real. It exists outside my brain.

I've been debating whether to go upriver with J.C. tomorrow. Part of me thinks it would be crazy. Heading into the jungle with that thing after me, in search of an *akij* who doesn't want to be found? But I can't stay here and do nothing, I'll go mad.

I've reached the end of this journal: only half a page left. Maybe that's a sign. One way or the other, I don't think I'll be writing any more. Tomorrow I will *make* J.C. take me to Kayun. Kayun is my only hope.

Twenty-Nine

An overcast morning, the forest steamily hot – and quiet. Muddy underfoot, the ground littered with fallen branches, trees dripping overhead. Earlier, as we pushed through the sodden vegetation, I put on my mac, but within moments I was sweating, so I took it off again and stuffed it in my rucksack. I move in a whining swarm of mosquitoes. As quickly as I spray on the DEET, it washes off.

We've just laboured up a steep ridge to the chatter of some unseen stream, then down into a tangled valley where we've paused for a breather at a spring. It's a beautiful spot, the water clear as amber, pimenta palms dripping with cats' claw vines studded with yellow flowers. We're crouching amid ferns of vivid rain-washed green, noisy with frogs. In the distance I can hear the boom of a waterfall. It's been with us all morning.

I've hardly had a moment to think since we left camp, and as I hunker on my haunches, watching sunlight and leaf-shadow on the water, that thing in the Mess feels like a bad dream.

J.C. is squatting beside me, gazing peacefully at the

water and picking his teeth with his thumbnail. Now's my chance.

'J.C.,' I say casually. 'Your uncle hasn't been to work for the past few days. Where's he gone?'

He examines his thumbnail. 'I don't know,' he mumbles, avoiding my eyes.

'Mr Ridley says he's not in the village. Is that true?'

The boy shrugs.

'Does that mean yes, or no?'

'I don't know, Dr Corbett. I think he's busy.'

'Doing what?'

He gives me a smile that's pathetic in its attempt to pla-cate. 'Dr Corbett, we don't ask an *akij* what he's doing.'

'But. J.C. – I have to ask. I have to talk to him.'

His handsome face contracts. 'I'm sorry,' he murmurs. 'I don't know.'

'Yes you do,' I gently insist. 'And you're going to tell me. I need to see him.'

'Why?' he says unhappily, casting about as if the jungle might come to his aid.

'Because he can help me. No one else can.'

'I'm sorry, Dr Corbett, I don't... He doesn't want to see you.'

I lean towards him, forcing him to meet my eyes. 'J.C. – I won't take no for an answer. You will take me to him.'

He is twisting his hands, those smooth child-like hands. I should pity him. I'm putting him in an impossible pos-ition. I don't care.

All at once his face clears, as if he's come to a decision. 'OK,' he mutters. 'Tomorrow. I'll take you tomorrow.'

*

Now that he's decided to help me we're back to our easy camaraderie. What's more, my senses are almost normal again and he's been spotting things before me, that's helping too.

I couldn't face returning to camp just yet and I thought a few hours' work might steady me, so we continued up the valley, then climbed another ridge into another valley, where J.C. heard a commotion in the distance. On going to investigate, we watched a troupe of spider monkeys trying to raid a macaws' nest and being driven off; J.C. and I exchanged grins.

After that we found a stand of hog plums. I've just spent two hours searching for mantids, so absorbed that I've hardly thought of anything else – and my search has paid off! With a lucky swipe of my net I've caught my first mantis! A gorgeous female *Acontista*, elegant green and white markings and spectacular, bulging, purple-pink eyes. I am *inordinately* pleased. Perhaps she's a sign that my luck has changed. Perhaps the jungle has forgiven me for fogging those ceibas.

And would you believe it, I've gone and left every last killing jar in the dugout?

She's my first mantis, I *can't* let her go. And where there is one, there may be more. It's not far to the river, plenty of time for J.C. to run and fetch a few jars and hurry back, while I stay here and continue the search. I can't let these hog plums out of my sight, at least not yet. And I can't risk going with J.C. and not being able to find them again.

To my relief he doesn't object to leaving me on my own. Perhaps he's realised that I'm not as helpless as I look.

*

Four o'clock and no sign of J.C., so I'm heading back to the river, marking my way with twists of grass tied to vines, to help me find those hog plums again. My captive mantis is scrabbling angrily in the too-small specimen bottle I found for her in my rucksack. Damn J.C. When I catch up with him I shall give him a piece of my mind.

The spring where we rested this morning looks different because one of the palm trees has fallen across it, burying the ferns beneath a tangle of vines. The frogs are still gamely piping. On the slope beyond, I spot a big copal tree that looks familiar, and start towards it. Not far now. Over the next ridge is that noisy little stream leading down to the river, and twenty minutes after that I'll be at the dugout. What's keeping that wretched boy?

As I crest the ridge I pause at the top and take off my hat. A damp wind lifts my hair, cooling my forehead. Before me and all around rise rank upon rank of green forested hills, their jagged heads misted with cloud.

With a twinge of disquiet it comes to me that I can no longer hear that waterfall. When did it fade out of earshot?

I think back to the spring I've just left, with its fallen palm. My stomach drops. That spring appeared different from the one where we rested this morning because it was. It was not the same spring.

Carefully, deliberately, I turn my head in every direction. I try to re-trace my steps. Can't find a single twist of grass tied to a vine. In fact I can't remember when I last bothered to fasten one. I wasn't paying attention.

Carefully, deliberately, I wipe my palms down my thighs. I suck in my lips. Again I cast about. I recognise nothing.

I have no idea which way to go.

Thirty

Lost in the jungle. Such a bloody cliché. I've read the sto-
ries in the Sunday supplements, I've seen the documenta-
ries on TV. Missionaries skewered by hostile Indians. Plane
crash survivors battling caimans, jaguars, snakes. Back-
packers going missing without a trace – until years later,
when someone stumbles across a pathetic scattering of
bones.

'J.C.!' I yell.

The green immensity returns no answer. Wherever
I turn I'm mocked by jagged hills and drifting clouds of
vapour. No rivers, no sign of humanity, no woodsmoke to
indicate a loggers' camp or an Indian village. I'm the only
human being in an endless wilderness of trees.

My thoughts scrabble like beetles in a jar. I picture my
journal locked in the tea chest in the lab. Is it good or bad
that it's not on my desk where someone could find it? If they
did, they would think I was mad and come after me. Since
they can't, they might assume I've simply gone off on my
own for a few days. *That's Corbett, always flouting the rules.*

If only I had a whistle. Ridley said it was 'Camp Regs' to
carry one, but I never bothered, I dismissed it as another

of the Professor's ludicrous rules. I wonder if that's going to prove fatal.

All this flashes through my mind in an instant, then I'm back to reality. I have no map. No idea where I am.

But I do know that the river flows roughly east to west. And on our previous forays J.C. and I have always headed uphill, *away* from the river; which must mean north. We did the same today. Therefore to find the river and the dugout I need to head south.

So where is south? The sky is overcast, I can't see the sun. Compass, you idiot. I unzip my trouser pocket and take it out, try to hold it steady on my palm. The tiny needle trembles – then points south, at a ferociously tangled slope looming above me. It's almost sheer. A monkey might be able reach the top. I haven't a hope.

'J.C.! Where are you!'

Not even an echo comes back. The jungle doesn't care.

'J.C.!' My voice cracks. I sound reedy and helpless.

I won't call again.

J.C. didn't object when I sent him off to fetch those killing jars, he went almost eagerly. At the time I thought this meant he believes I can look after myself. Now I wonder. Perhaps he never intended to return. Perhaps he's abandoned me.

That moment at the spring when I pressed him to take me to Kayun and his face suddenly cleared. I assumed he'd decided to help me. But what if I'm wrong? What if he's never forgiven me for fogging those ceibas? What if Kayun put him up to this? *Take the ts'ul into the jungle and leave him.*

No. I refuse to believe that J.C. would do that. We work well together, we're almost friends.

Besides, he must know that he couldn't get away with it. How would he explain returning to camp without me? As soon as he arrived they'd send out a search party. So he *can't* have abandoned me, it doesn't make sense.

Then why am I worrying?

Because maybe J.C. won't return to camp and raise the alarm. He's an intelligent boy, he knows what will happen if he turns up alone. And he doesn't have to. It would be easy for him to hide out in the jungle, pretend he got lost trying to find me, then make his way back to camp in his own sweet time. He'll only have to hide out for a few days, he knows I won't last long. By the time he does finally raise the alarm, I'll be finished. And dead men tell no tales.

Is this panicky fantasy, or an accurate assessment of my predicament?

I picture J.C.'s handsome features, as unknowable as a Maya carving. What accident of chromosomal shuffling produced such purity, when so many of his relations are deformed or cross-eyed?

The ancient Maya regarded crossed eyes as a sign of beauty. They fostered it by dangling little balls between their babies' eyes. They also squeezed the soft infant skulls between boards, to create that weirdly flattened profile. How could one ever understand such people? What do I really know about J.C.?

My mind is wandering, I don't have time for this. In a couple of hours it'll be dark. Part of that slope looks a little less impossible. I need to get moving.

*

A fallen tree blocks my way. Hacking and slashing at branches with my machete, I scramble over the trunk, and as I jump down the other side something slithers past my boot. *Fuck, Simon, remember to look where you put your feet!*

'Clueless, clueless,' I pant as I stop to check the compass. I'm shocked to find that I haven't been heading south, but *east*. The jungle has been forcing me off course, even further into the wilderness.

It's twenty past four, less than two hours till dark. What am I doing, blundering about? *Stop!* Assess your gear. Even the humblest Boy Scout knows that.

As a boy I shunned the Boy Scouts. I detested the companionship and the rivalry over badges. Edwin adored all that. If he were here now he'd be in his element. He would know what to do.

I pat my breast pocket. The talisman. The feel of it steadies me a little. I decide to take stock.

I have my machete and my Swiss Army knife, thank God. Compass (for what it's worth), waterproof wristwatch, lighters, torch, plastic mac. I can rig it up as a tent; I can use the fishing line and hooks too. Shame I don't have a mosquito net, but it can't be helped, at least I've got DEET. And a basic first aid kit, though no anti-snakebite serum (we won't think about that). The binoculars are heavy but worth keeping, if I spot a helicopter I can flash signals, surely even I can manage that? As long as it's sunny, of course. If it's cloudy, binoculars will be so much dead weight. Unfortunate turn of phrase.

What else have I got? Field guides aren't much use but I can't bear to chuck them, not yet. Toilet paper ditto, for now it stays. Same goes for the *Acontista* in her specimen bottle. She's cost me blood and tears to find, I'm damned if I'm giving her up now.

No food. Another beginner's mistake. Every survival manual decrees that you should always, *always* carry emergency provisions. Still, a day or so without food won't kill me. And surely I can find something to eat?

The water bottle is another worry, it's only a third full. But come on, this is a rainforest, I'm not going to die of thirst. At the bottom of my pack I find something that startles me: the little glass tube containing what remains of the *muktan*. How did that get into my rucksack? Last time I saw it I was locking it in the tea chest. I have no recollection of taking it out.

Half past four. I'm wasting time. Think logically. What do I need to get through the night?

Shelter. Fire. Water. Food. Yes. Let's get going.

'There now,' I tell the jungle. 'Not so bad for a beginner. You've got shelter and firewood. Now off we go to find water and something to eat.' Talking to myself is weirdly comforting. I read somewhere that morale is essential to surviving in the wild.

I've built my tent on the only flattish ground I could find, after checking for ant nests and dead wood that might harbour snakes. I've bent a sapling horizontal and tied it to another sapling with fishing line to make a crossbeam. Over this I've tented my mac, securing its edges to the surrounding vegetation with more fishing line threaded through the buttonholes, plus a few hastily cut stakes.

Dry firewood has been a problem. Having searched

in vain, I've felled a young balsa tree and split a piece lengthways to get at the dry(ish) wood inside. I've also felled a small palm and scrounged the dead fronds on its crown. I've stacked everything inside the tent in case it rains while I'm away.

Half-past five, not long till dusk – but no downpours as yet, thank Christ. I'm terrified of losing my way, so I've cut a length of liana, and every few paces I tie a knot of twisted fibre to a branch: at eye level, where I'll be sure to see it. It heartens me that I've thought of this. It means I'm not losing my nerve.

I come to a strangler fig smothering a copal, but the unripe fruits are pebble-hard. I find a fallen palm and search the bark for weevil grubs, remembering J.C. smacking his lips. No grubs, only empty pupa casings and a few big adult weevils which I can't bring myself to eat.

Something stirs at the corner of my vision. A grasshopper on a leaf. It's five inches long and green, no brilliant colours warning of poison. I catch it easily, twist off its head and zip the body in my pocket for later.

Water is becoming a worry, but I can't find a stream or even a puddle, and the epiphytes with their mosquito-filled reservoirs are hopelessly out of reach in the trees. When I pause to pee, I'm alarmed to see that my urine is already dark orange; almost the colour of *muktan*. How like me to become dehydrated in a rainforest. And how ironic that my heightened perceptions should desert me just when I could have used them to find a stream.

Once or twice on our forays, J.C. chopped off a segment of bamboo and water gushed out, drinkable, if tasting of chlorophyll. He told me that only one species of bamboo stores water this way, you have to look for the canes which are bent by the weight.

Of course I can't find any, and after hacking at the wrong kind of bamboo I've rubbed my hand raw between finger and thumb. It hurts like the devil; and that bite in the crook of my elbow is itching again. It's the size of a golf ball. I hope it's not infected, that's all I need.

I'm about to turn back when I hear the screeches of parrots. Parrots love fruit. I blunder towards the sound – *not* forgetting to mark my way.

Success! The birds are gorging high in some tree I don't recognise, its branches are laden with yellow fruit. Spider monkeys are also feasting. If my fellow primates can eat that fruit, surely I can too?

I riffle the leaf litter for windfalls. What I find is the size of a plum, and a virulent yellow. Flicking off ants, I nibble the pulpy flesh. Deliciously sweet, I gobble the rest. I find five more, bruised and brown with decay. Reverently I store them in my rucksack for later.

I'm halfway back to the shelter when a morpho butterfly as big as my hand flashes past, an otherworldly shimmer of metallic turquoise and velvety black.

The Yachikel believe that morphos are reincarnated spirits which lure people to their doom. That makes me think of the butterflies on Penelope's frock the night we met. My throat closes, and suddenly to my horror I'm on the verge of tears. 'Not here, you wimp,' I growl. I don't know if my tears are for her or for me.

I stayed too long under that tree gathering fruit. Dusk is falling fast, and it's still twenty minutes to my tent.

Ten minutes later it's night, and eerily quiet. No wind, no rain, no frogs. Only a subdued rasp of crickets and the leathery thwap of a bat.

I snap on my torch. The beam reveals fire ants swarming up a vine. A spider's multifaceted stare. I move warily, watching where I place my feet. I dread catching the green eyeshine of a jaguar.

Sure enough, I get the creeping feeling of being watched. I picture the great cat silently stalking. Like all predators it selects prey which is sick, tired, weak. I see myself as the jaguar sees me: a puny, defenceless creature tottering blindly in a glare of its own making.

Directly ahead, something big moves in the dark. Eyes throw back the torchlight. I yelp. A guinea pig the size of a wild boar crashes off into the gloom.

I bark a jittery laugh. Capybara. *Damn.* If I'd been quick with my machete my food worries would be over.

Breathing through my mouth, I stumble on. My encounter with the capybara has made me feel a bit better. It's encouraging to know that another creature is as terrified as I.

Time to make a fire and roast that grasshopper.

Thirty-One

No wonder people worship fire. I worship it too: sitting on my rucksack and staring in adoration at the crackling, leaping flames.

For a clueless non-Boy Scout I'm doing pretty well. I've rigged up a shelter and I have fire. *I have fire.* That makes me feel like a god.

True, I miss my hammock and my mosquito net and I'm unpleasantly vulnerable, seated on the bare ground which I've cleared with my machete, my eyes on stalks for scorpions and snakes. But so far all I've encountered are beetles and a rather splendid bird-eating spider; I scooped her up on a palm frond and relocated her to the leaf litter a few yards away.

While I was doing that, I spotted a nest of leaf-cutter ants. Above ground the nest is merely a naked mound of earth, but underneath there will be a subterranean metropolis of tunnels. I like to picture it, it's a kind of company.

My grasshopper wasn't half bad. Mexicans fry them in oil and salt but I had to make do with roasting. It went bright red, like a miniature lobster; similar consistency, though admittedly not as nice. I saved the plums or whatever they are till last. They were staggeringly delicious. And so far, no diarrhoea or other ill effects.

Since then I've been checking myself for bites and scratches. I was surprised to find that my hands and forearms are covered in red welts, they're only now beginning to hurt. Odd that I didn't feel them before. Presumably that's down to adrenaline. I didn't feel the thorns either. They've gone right through my trousers into my flesh, it's taken ages to tweezer them out.

The bite in the crook of my arm is now the size of a plum. Bot fly maggot, like the one the doctor squeezed out of Ridley's back. I've tried to pop it but it hurt abominably and refused to burst. I can see the worm's tiny red breathing hole on top. When I block it with my finger, I feel the maggot squirming in my flesh.

My right hand is the worst. Hours of wielding the machete have made it a raw, blistered mess. I've no means of cleaning it, I can only sprinkle on powdered sulphur and bandage it with gauze. That'll have to do.

Patching myself up has been painful, but steadying. I have restored order, therefore self-respect. I am no longer a defenceless little mammal, I am human again. Ashamed of my earlier panic – and contrite about J.C. Poor lad's probably frantic with worry; either searching for me on his own, or else he's made it back to camp and is raising the alarm. Maybe they've already mounted a search party. If not, they'll come looking for me as soon as it's light. I shall have to keep a sharp lookout for planes.

As for water – heck, even if I can't find a stream, it's bound to rain soon. I can lick it off leaves.

*

Just now I poked my head out of the tent. The sky is clear: a hot, bright, moonlit night. Too bright for the jungle's nocturnal inhabitants, that's why it's so quiet. No shrieks or rustlings, which is a relief. Even the frogs sound muted. No wind either. And no rain.

That's why the fireflies are out. In the gloom I glimpse their magical greenish-yellow flickering. Mating dance. I've seen it in Jamaica, I find it beautiful and sad. In the old days, planters' wives used to pin them alive to the hems of their ballgowns. The things people do.

I add another chunk of balsa wood to the fire and it settles with a hiss, sending a flurry of sparks into the canopy.

I take the talisman from my breast pocket. Unwrap it, turn it in my fingers. Firelight gleams on Penelope's dark hair.

All those different 'looks' of hers. The swinging chick, the demure secretary, the beatnik rebel in combat gear. The ethereal princess clothed in butterflies. I realise now that she was doing more than trying out 'looks'. She was experimenting with different versions of herself. Trying to work out who she would become.

She treated me badly. I see that now. Leading me on, rebuffing me, calling me back. That scarf I bought for her. Jacintha was telling the truth. I can imagine Penelope sending me up to her friends, laughing her rich robust laugh. *Old lady chic.* It makes me shrivel inside.

And yet how can I blame her? Beauty had given her awesome power and she didn't know how to use it. She was too young. Jeremy was wrong, she wasn't a prick-tease. She wasn't that calculating. She simply didn't

understand the effect she had on men. She was thought-
less and selfish and let's face it, not very bright. But that
doesn't change anything. I still love her.

I've been alone my whole life. All it took was a few
kind words at a drinks party, some butterflies on a frock,
a beautiful face – and wham, my pent-up feelings found
their target. Unstoppable. A heat-seeking missile.

God I was an idiot. I truly believed that we were soul-
mates. Terrifying how reason flew out of the window.

Did I cause her death? I can't believe that my letter rattled her that much. Surely she simply crumpled it up and
thought no more about it? But what happened in the car
park...

Her hair was loose that night. As we struggled, a lock of
it snagged on my wristwatch; I think that's what happened, though I wasn't aware of it at the time, and as she
yanked herself free I must have inadvertently pulled it out.
That's why she screamed. I didn't even realise until she'd
driven off and I saw her hair tangled in my fist. The tiny
bead of blood at the end of the follicle.

I wrote in my journal that I made the talisman from
strands caught on a twig, but that was a lie, I made it from
the hair I took from her that night. She was shaken and in
pain. I saw the patch of bright blood at her temple as she
drove off. Was that what made her attempt that bend too
fast? Was it?

Just now when I replaced the talisman in my pocket, I
came across something else: the little glass tube that
holds the remains of the *muktan*. In the firelight it glows
ruby red.

I've no intention of taking the vile stuff again, and yet I can't bring myself to chuck it. Earlier I even transferred it from my rucksack to my breast pocket, so that I wouldn't sit on it. I don't know why.

I used to think that *muktan* was my last link with Penelope. Instead it opened a door and let something out. Kayun's brother. The nameless, faceless *akij* who – if Ridley's hunch is correct – slit his own throat. '*And other things.*'

Perhaps Ridley is right, and the Indian believed he would be with the gods if he died a violent death; that he would gain the power to protect whatever it was he held sacred. What intensity of feeling had he reached, what pitch of desperation, to cut his own throat?

His ancestors believed that everyone else – all those who didn't die by violence – were doomed to Xibalba, the Place of Fear. It had different levels, each with its own horrors; like the House of Blades, where obsidian knives fly about looking for something to cut. For the Maya, hell had nothing to do with sin. It didn't matter what you'd done in life. Unless you died by violence, you couldn't escape.

Again the fire settles with a hiss. The sky has clouded over. Darkness presses on me from all sides.

Thirty-Two

When you're thirsty it's all you think about. Your body clamours for water. It knows it won't last long. What's the saying? Three weeks without food, three days without water, three minutes without air.

Mid-morning and hot, I'm struggling through the densest understorey yet. So far, I've heard no planes.

The howlers woke me before dawn. They sounded as if they were out to get me. I'd spent a grim night huddled by the fire, flinching whenever a branch snapped or a shadow moved. Once I started awake to find my scalp burning, flames running all over my skin. It was an hour before I'd killed the last leaf-cutter ant and by then I was covered in stinging welts. Simon, you bloody fool. Why did you camp so close to that nest?

A splash to my left. My heart leaps. Water!

There's another splash. Wildly I attack the undergrowth, wielding my machete awkwardly in my left hand. It's a good sign that the vegetation's so thick, it always is near water.

From the direction of the splashing comes the chatter of kiskadees and the screech of parakeets – then with startling suddenness I'm breaking through into sunlight.

Before me lies a strip of dazzling white sand – and beyond it *the river*. Its sluggish black water is barely visible beneath overhanging trees, floating branches and the huge sludge-green pads of giant waterlilies. I've never seen anything more beautiful.

The water is cloudy and smells rank, two days ago I wouldn't have touched it. Now I drop to my knees and drink. I fill my water bottle, drink more. Who cares about tapeworms and those tiny fish that eat you from the inside? You've got to be alive to play host to parasites.

Swallows skim the waterlilies, dragonflies flash past. I catch the jade-green flicker of a kingfisher. A turtle plops off the trunk of a fallen tree that spans the river, and an iguana watches me from a nearby rock. Before I can think about killing it, it slips beneath the surface. *Nil desperandum*, where there's water there's life. I have found the river. I am saved. Now all I have to do is head downstream. I'm bound to find help.

After a couple of hundred yards I come to a bend in the river. No, not a bend, a wall of impenetrable dark-green vegetation. The river has disappeared. It simply isn't there any more.

Puzzled, I backtrack along the sand – two, three, four hundred yards. Another dead end blocks my way.

A horrible suspicion occurs to me. I cut off a philodendron leaf and toss it in the water. The leaf rocks, then goes still. No current to carry it away.

I feel as if I'm falling. This isn't the river. It's a lake.

*

'*Fuck!*'

The birds cease their chatter at this strange new sound. '*Fuck, fuck, fuck!*' I fling down my rucksack.

Out in the lake, something sinks out of sight. A breeze ruffles the surface, sending waterlight rippling up the overhanging trunks. Then the breeze dies and the stillness returns. The stillness of the jungle at noon. Leaves waxy with heat, forest creatures hiding from the sun. All I can hear is the buzz and hum of insects.

Savagely I slap at mosquitoes. My DEET's running low, but I'm saving it for tonight. I stare with loathing at the vast blue empty sky. No planes. But what did I expect? Even if J.C. did raise the alarm within hours of my going missing – even if the Professor has radioed for help – the nearest plane is hundreds of miles away in San Cristóbal. If they can persuade it to come.

Now that I'm no longer thirsty, hunger comes roaring back. I find a bush laden with tempting scarlet berries, but I've no idea what they are and I can't see anything eating them, so they're not worth the risk.

In the lake a fish leaps. I've never caught a fish in my life. I'm not going to waste time and energy trying.

A swarm of sulphur butterflies is feeding on some tracks criss-crossing the sand. I walk with my head down, trying to decipher the prints. Many animals have come to the water to drink. I make out the delicate fretwork of bird feet, and tapirs' three-toed prints. The tiny hoof-marks of deer.

I've almost reached the lake's eastern end when I catch a gamey smell that reminds me of the Big Cat House at the zoo. Before me in the sand are several large, confident paw-marks. I picture the jaguar crouching in the under-growth, an easy pounce from where I stand. I move back into the open.

According to my compass, in order to head south I need to cross this bloody lake, then find a way up yet another forbiddingly steep ridge. The lake is about sixty feet wide, and almost spanned by that fallen tree, its trunk a half-submerged tangle of jutting branches clogged with vines. I picture snakes and poisonous frogs. Caimans. Piranhas. Electric eels. I step onto the tree trunk and start across.

The trunk is soft with decay, it's crumbling and lurching, water slopping into my boots. To hell with watching where you put your hands, I'm clutching any branch I can reach to keep from falling off.

I'm almost at the other side when the trunk rolls and pitches me into the lake.

I come up spluttering, clawing lilypads. Fuck, even the waterlilies bite, the undersides of the pads are cover-ed in spikes. The lake bottom is squelchy, it sucks at my boots. As I flounder for the shore I catch a disorientating close-up of shiny black spinning seeds, inches from my face. Whirligig beetles. With each eye they can see both above the surface and below: two worlds at the same time; like Kayun. Heaving myself out, I collapse panting on the sand.

Mosquitoes descend in a cloud, blackening my skin. Snarling, I blast them with more precious DEET.

A sharp pain in my calf, and I'm just too late to swat a deer fly. And oh Christ, I've lost my hat in the lake. I also forgot to zip my rucksack. My field guide and toilet paper are a sodden mess, ditto the first aid kit, I forgot to zip that too. Luckily my lighter is safe in its waterproof tin and somehow I kept hold of my machete, but I've lost my knife. Stupid, *stupid*.

My binoculars are still hanging round my neck like a stone. Should I ditch them? But if a plane did come, I'd have no way to signal. Better keep them for now.

A whimper rises in my throat. Every choice I make is fraught with significance. It might determine if I live or die.

Something's tickling my left knee. Rolling up my trouser leg, I find a rusty-red leech the size of my thumb, bloated with my blood. Grimacing, I rip the thing off – recalling too late that that's exactly what you shouldn't do. Sure enough, the head remains with its teeth sunk in my flesh. I dig it out with tweezers and grind it between two stones: take that, you little bastard.

A body search reveals six more of the ghastly creatures, including one on my groin. How is this possible, when I was only in the water a few minutes?

Because, you idiot, they didn't all come from the lake, you've been wading through wet foliage for hours. Your body heat is a clarion call to feed.

In films when the hero slashes his way through the jungle, he sustains at most a decorous cut on the cheekbone, which merely accentuates the manly planes of his face – and which of course he stoically ignores. Every single one of my bites and scratches hurts, and they've just been soaked in filthy water. I have never felt so vulnerable. Every tiny lesion in my flesh is an open invitation to microbes, fungi, parasites, urine, scat, plant and animal toxins and the poisonous products of decay.

What's the use of my brain being vastly more powerful than that of any other creature in the forest when my body is so pathetically weak, my skin so easily bitten, pierced, stung? Why should this be? Is it evolution's sick joke? What a piece of work is a man.

Stop whining, Simon. This isn't going to find the river. It's time to tackle that ridge.

I'm struggling uphill when I catch the clamour of spider monkeys. By the sound of them they're not far off. Maybe they've found one of those trees with the delicious yellow fruit.

Yes! The undergrowth beneath their tree is spattered with droppings and reeks of piss, and the monkeys are messy feeders, tossing down twigs and half-eaten fruit. I find one in the leaf litter, wipe it on my sleeve, cram it in my mouth. The next one is covered in flies, probably riddled with larvae. Who cares, it's only added protein.

The monkeys have seen me. Shrieking and jumping up and down, they shake branches and pelt me with sticks.

'Fuck off!' I yell, scrabbling for more fruit.

A jet of piss narrowly misses my head. A few feet above me, the leaves part and a furry wizened face peers down. For a moment our eyes lock, and I meet the monkey's alien consciousness. Its life is eating, mating, fighting and fleeing. Nothing else. No awareness of self, no knowledge that it must die. And yet it knows the jungle better than I ever will.

Baring its long yellow teeth, it hurls a branch at my head. I catch the branch and chuck it back as hard as I can. 'Go away!' I roar. 'This is *my* tree!'

Screaming, the monkey beats the trunk with its fist.

Spider monkeys are cowards. One shout from me should be enough to send the whole troupe flying through the canopy. But not this time. More monkeys are swarming down the trunk, screeching at me and flinging sticks.

I run. So much for higher consciousness.

The ancient Maya believed that monkeys are what's left from the gods' previous, botched attempt at making men. The wooden people were a mistake, so the gods set the whole world against them. They were maimed, burnt, torn limb from limb, eyes gouged out – and those that survived took to the trees and became monkeys. Maybe that's why they hate us.

I leave them behind and struggle up the ridge, my hand hurting viciously, my feet squelching and blistered.

It comes to me that those monkeys showed no fear. Does that mean they've never been hunted? That they've never seen men?

Thirty-Three

I've made it to the top of the ridge. The compass says I'm facing south, but below me the forest falls away into yet another deep valley, with no sign of the river.

Further down my side of the valley, an outcrop of grey rocks pokes through the trees like bones. Beside it a giant ceiba rears its head above the canopy. *No river.* Shutting my mind to what this means, I start down the slope.

As soon as I enter the forest I sense that it's different. The trees are taller, the canopy denser, the heat more intense. It's three in the afternoon, yet I'm walking in dim green twilight. Above me unseen birds utter shrill, echoing cries. Ridley once said that there are some valleys where not even Indians dare go. *Too many spirits.* I wish I hadn't remembered that.

I'm shaky with hunger and dizzy with fatigue. My feet are a pulpy mess of blisters, every step hurts. Thorns catch at my clothes and my boots scuff leaf litter, releasing an earthy smell of mould. Behind me something rustles. Glancing over my shoulder, I blunder into the hanging snares of cats' claw vines.

The undergrowth erupts and I jump a mile. Whatever it

is crashes past, and I glimpse a large dappled rump and a pig-like snout. Tapir, I tell myself, drawing deep slow breaths. Only a tapir.

Above me three fruit bats hang upside-down from a branch, like furred brown pods. The nearest one scratches its chin with a black claw and peers down at me. *What are you doing here? You don't belong.*

The gloom deepens. The birds have fallen silent. The heat is thick in my throat. Bad weather on the way. I need to find somewhere to camp.

Not far off, a tree groans. Birds shoot shrieking into the sky. There's a rushing sound like wind, then a crash, alarmingly close, and the ground beneath my feet shudders. Not far from where I stand, grey sunlight slants down, where before there was shadow.

Great trees are meant to fall. It's how the forest renews itself, their ruin letting in light for seedlings to grow, their decay feeding insects and fungi. I know that. But standing here in this preternatural gloom, it feels personal. Trees have become the enemy. They will kill me if they can.

Swaying with exhaustion, I stand between two of the ceiba's huge buttressed roots. High above me the great tree spreads enormous limbs that drip with vines and bristle with epiphytes and ferns.

Some trees have more presence than others. This one is taller than any I've encountered – and older, not many spikes on its trunk, which is entwined with epiphyte roots snaking down to the forest floor. I have fogged six of its sisters. I wonder if it knows. I wouldn't dream of fogging this one. It emanates a sense of a life unreachably different from my own. Awareness without consciousness. Strength without intent.

The ancient Maya valued green things more than gold. Jade, turquoise, the quetzal bird's iridescent blue-green feathers. They believed that a giant ceiba stands at the centre of the world. It grows from a caiman's spiny back, and in its topmost branches perches a scarlet macaw.

When I first read that I thought it surprisingly benign for a people steeped in blood. Pragmatic too, since forests do mean life. But now, alone with this monster, it doesn't feel like a myth. It feels like the truth.

The obvious place to camp is here between its roots, which enclose me like walls. I could rig up a roof of bamboo and palm fronds, use my mac as a groundsheet.

But. The wind is rising and clouds are massing. A storm isn't far off. If there's lightning, camping under the tallest tree in the forest could prove fatal.

A few yards to the east, that outcrop of iron-grey boulders juts skywards like broken teeth. I could make a shelter in there. Yes, and doubtless plenty of snakes and scorpions have had the same idea.

So what's it to be, Simon? Snakebite or lightning strike?

Lightning every time, at least it'll be quick.

From where I stand, the ground drops steeply, giving a clear view across the valley to the opposite ridge. Above it the sky has darkened to pewter. The trees on the ridge blaze luminous green. The storm will come from there.

A mosquito whines in my ear. The heat is stifling, it lies on my flesh like a second skin.

Further up the valley, the howlers begin to roar.

Thirty-Four

Every creature in the forest knows the storm isn't far off. Monkeys flying from branch to branch, crows scudding for cover like scraps of burnt paper.

I'm scrabbling in the outcrop, gathering sticks for a fire. The wind is rattling the pimenta palms and flattening the bamboo beyond the rocks; across the valley, thunder is growling, lightning flickering as if someone were switching a lamp on and off. As I pause for breath, a blazing white cord spears the ridge, then there's a rippling crack of thunder and the ridge disappears behind an iron-grey wall of rain.

Clutching my firewood, I struggle back to the ceiba. Around me trees are groaning, branches snapping and crashing. Below me the valley is a churning green chaos, and that grey wall is sweeping towards me and I still have no roof.

I race back to the pimentas, hack off ten-foot fronds and bamboo canes. A blinding flash of lightning, and in the mud beneath the bamboo I spot a dead parakeet. It's un-scavenged, still limp, maybe killed by a hawk. I stuff the carcase inside my shirt and haul the vegetation back to the ceiba.

I improvise a tepee, propping palm fronds against the trunk and steadying them with bamboo canes planted crosswise; I lash them to the tree's spikes with fishing line. My tepee is only just big enough to take me, with a small fire in front. As I fight to get it going, I ask the tree's permission to camp between its feet. I wish I'd done that sooner.

At first the rain is a low hiss in the canopy below, but it quickly swells to a roar. It takes a few minutes to penetrate the ceiba's foliage, then suddenly it's hammering onto my tepee with annihilating force. I'm cold. Forget the groundsheet, I wriggle into my mac; I should have done that before I got wet. Débris is clattering into the undergrowth. I flinch at every dazzle of lightning, every crash of thunder. The storm has intent. It's out to get me.

Now for the parakeet. I pluck it as best I can and claw out the guts, skewer the scrawny carcase on a stick and set it to roast.

Some hope. The fire is dead. I give up and gnaw the tough flesh raw, wolfing it with cave-man grunts, sucking blood off my fingers.

The Maya were right. Blood is life.

Ten to six, and already dark.

Gradually, the interval between lightning and thunder lengthens and the flashes become less blinding. Now the thunder is growling in the distance, the rain diminishing to a steady downpour. It's no longer out to get me. I can't believe it. My tepee has defied the onslaught. I mutter my thanks to the tree.

I'm thirsty again and my water bottle's been empty for

hours, but that shouldn't be a problem. Flicking on my torch, I head out into the rain.

As soon as I leave the shelter of the ceiba it's coming down so hard it stings my face and the backs of my hands. Through the billowing grey curtains the boulders are hunched figures. I don't like the way they seem to come and go. How many are there? Seven? No, six. No, seven. Definitely seven.

That's when I notice the water streaming down their flanks. Why didn't I think of that before? You need a drink? Well, there it is.

With no means of collecting it, I lick rain straight off the nearest boulder. God, what a relief. It has a metallic tang of iron, and already I feel strength coursing through me.

After drinking my fill, I scurry back to camp. I've no fire and I'm chilled to the bone, but I've built a shelter and survived the storm, I have found food and water. For an amateur I'm not doing too badly.

On impulse I rummage in my rucksack for the specimen bottle. Astonishingly, the *Acontista* is still alive. Again I snap on my torch and venture out, clutching the specimen bottle. This time I head away from the rocks.

A few yards from the ceiba I get lucky and blunder into a hog plum. Good, she'll feel at home in that. Gently I shake her onto a sheltered branch. Then with a length of fishing line I tie the specimen bottle to another branch. It might serve as a sign if a rescue party passes this way. I'm glad I thought of that, it shows I'm still thinking logically.

The mantis is an offering to propitiate the spirits. Like that time after I'd collected the *muktan* orchids, when I opened the killing jars and freed the insects.

If this was a fairy tale, those insects would be grateful, they would come to my aid. But that's not how things work. I used to look down on the early explorers, with their 'Man against Nature' attitude. But standing in the rain beside the hog plum, I realise they were right. The jungle *is* against me. That's the truth. It's how things are. I am not Yachikel. I don't belong here. We white men left Eden a long time ago, of our own accord. We can never go back.

The hog plum is only a few yards from the ceiba, but as soon as I return I know that something has changed. Someone has been in my camp. I have a vivid impression of movement, furtively stilled. Like the feeling you get when you enter a house which you thought was empty, but you realise it's not, that someone is hiding inside.

Nothing has been disturbed and I can find no trace of monkeys. I know it's not monkeys. Wrapping my mac tighter, I huddle by the sodden firewood. The wind has died to a chill breeze, the rain is steadily falling. I can feel that I'm being watched.

Switching on my torch, I play the beam at the rocks. Once again I count them. This time I always come up with the same number, but it's always wrong. Only six. Before there were seven. I know there were.

The feel of this place has changed. Or is it that I've only just noticed? The rocks, the ceiba, even the palms and the bamboo: all are actively hostile. I have *taken* shelter from this tree. I have *taken* water from the rocks. They gave me nothing. I shouldn't be here.

The rain diminishes to a hissing, whispering presence.

When I switch off the torch, the darkness is absolute. I shut my eyes. I am frightened of what I might see.

I wake with a jolt: from deep sleep to taut awareness in an instant. I can feel the hairs bristling on my scalp.

Huddled on my side, I lie in inky blackness. The rain has stopped. I hear dripping and trickling, the ringing calls of frogs. I can't work out where I am. Groping above me, my fingers claw air. Slowly I move my arm down towards the ground. My fingers touch sopping palm fronds. I seem to be lying half in and half out of what's left of the tepee.

In the distance, lightning flares, and for a moment it shows me the mottled wet bark of the ceiba's buttressed roots and above me the canopy, a black and emerald mosaic like shattered stained glass. My heart stops. Something is up there. It is crouching on the bough directly overhead. Time stretches. I make out its floating hair and the shadow where its face should be. I sense the horror of its ravaged throat. I feel its menace beating down at me.

The lightning blinks out. In the blackness I know that the thing has dropped to earth like a spider. It's behind me. I twist round. A leathery face touches mine, its mouth agape in a voiceless snarl.

Wheezing, I lurch to my feet. I blunder through thorns. Another flare of lightning. I glance over my shoulder.

It is standing beneath the ceiba. Arms by its sides. Watching me.

'I haven't done anything!' I cry as I crash through more thorns.

The ground drops sharply. I fall into nothingness.

Thirty-Five

I'm awake before the howlers: huddled against a log, hugging my knees. Silently begging the forest to emerge from the dark.

A dank grey dawn, islands of vapour floating among the trees. Kiskadees beginning to chatter, cicadas starting their monotonous rasp. Across the valley, the ridge is hidden by cloud. Below me lies a white sea of mist.

I'm cold and cramped. My scalp is crawling with barklice and other debris washed down from the canopy. I am drained by the aftermath of fear, yet strangely calm. Was I really that panicky creature who fled his camp and crashed down the slope? It feels as if it happened to someone else.

Gradually I become aware of the noise of running water, somewhere to my right. It sounds like a stream, and it's not far off. How did I miss that yesterday?

I realise I'm clutching a hank of mouldy straw. I've no memory of picking it up, no idea why I felt compelled to hang onto it all night.

In fact it isn't straw, it's woven from what appears to be palm fibre. It reminds me of the little woven creatures in

Kayun's hut, although this one is ant-eaten and blotched with mould; but there's no mistaking that sinuous shape, that flat serpentine head. It's a snake.

They're meant to be guardians, Ridley told me after my first visit to the Yachikel village. They put them on graves. I throw the thing in the undergrowth. I wipe my fingers down my thigh. I refuse to think about what this might mean.

As I struggle to my feet, I'm shocked to see how little ground I covered last night. Twenty yards above me, the ceiba comes and goes in the mist. I am intensely reluctant to climb back to it, but I need to retrieve my gear.

As I start uphill, something pale beneath a bush catches my eye. It's another palm-fibre creature. With the toe of my boot I turn it over. I can just make out the wide mouth and bulging eyes of a frog.

I search the leaf mould for more, hoping I won't find them. Knowing that I will. It doesn't take long to unearth the other two. They're tattered and gnawed, but I recognise the macaw by its beak, the jaguar by its spots. Four guardians to protect the four corners of a grave.

I'm beginning to feel sick. I don't want to face what this means, and yet my mind flashes back to what I did last night in the storm. I licked water off a boulder. I relished its strengthening tang of iron. But why iron? Those rocks are grey limestone, no iron in that. As I climb to the ceiba, I try to keep the implications at bay.

My tepee is a sodden mess of palm fronds. Among them I find my rucksack, machete, binoculars, water bottle. Surprisingly, my torch still works, although the batteries are getting low; it won't last much longer.

The clouds part, and beyond the ceiba the boulders gleam cold silver. I can't bear to find out if my suspicions are correct – and yet I have to know.

Shouldering my gear, I move towards them. Something makes me glance back. My stomach turns over. I didn't notice it last night, but one of the great tree's buttresses – the one facing the rocks – is spattered and stained. The stains are so dark they're almost black.

On the rock facing the ceiba – the one I licked last night – I make out traces of more dark splashes. My stomach convulses. I bend double with my hands on my knees and retch.

A lot of blood sprayed on the rocks. That's what Ridley said.

Kayun's brother. This is where he died.

Before leaving the ceiba, I unzip my pocket and bring out the little glass tube of *muktan*. Then I empty it onto the grave – or where I guess the grave may have been, although I've really no idea because scavengers have scattered its palm-fibre guardians.

'There,' I say aloud to whatever might be listening. 'That's the last of the *muktan*. Take it. I want nothing to do with it.'

I consider tying the empty tube to a branch as another sign for the rescue party, but instead I lob it down the slope. There's no point leaving a sign, I know that now. The rescue party isn't coming.

Did I pour out the *muktan* as an offering, to propitiate whatever haunts this place? I have no such illusions. I haven't forgotten the hatred in Kayun's eyes. *Always more white men. Taking our great trees. Destroying our sacred places. Taking. Always taking.* Hatred like that takes generations to grow. It's as deep as the leaf mould in the jungle. It feeds on itself.

I find the stream by its sound and drink, and refill my water bottle. I follow it downhill, determined not to let it out of my sight. I don't know whether it will lead me to the river – or if it does, whether it will be the right river, or else some nameless stream that will only lead me further from rescue – but that thought barely registers. I feel calm, even composed. I know I'm being hunted. And like all prey, I will do my utmost to escape.

High in a tree, a white hawk hitches itself into the sky and flies away. A lizard on a leaf freezes at my approach; as I pass, I am careful not to meet its eyes. I fear what I might see staring out at me. What haunts me used to be an *akij*. A shape-shifter. It can take any form.

Last night I shouted my innocence: 'I haven't *done* anything!'

That might be true, but it doesn't matter.

What haunts this place doesn't care what I have or haven't done. When it was alive, it slit its own throat – 'and other things'. It spattered its life across the rocks and the sacred tree.

Is that why it haunts?

Does it want the same for me?

Thirty-Six

Where did the stream go?

I've been following it all morning. Glimpsing it through undergrowth, hearing its rush and tumble down the slope – and now suddenly it isn't there. No bubbling chatter, no glint of water, nothing.

I backtrack to where I last saw it; then, slowly, I move downhill again. I catch a faint, echoing gurgle. It takes a moment to realise what this means. The stream has gone underground.

I am shocked by the depth of my disappointment. I've been counting on this little thread of water to lead me to the river. It's my only hope of rescue. And it appears that I do still hope to be rescued.

The ancient Maya believed that Xibalba, the land of the dead, lay underground. That's why they regarded caves as sacred. The Yachikel still do. *Xayaxché is finished*, Kayun said once. *We take money to protect what's left.* Maybe that's why his brother came out here to kill himself. If there is a sacred cave somewhere under my feet, maybe he wanted to end his life here, to become one with the gods: to protect it from white men. To stop it going the same way as all the other ancient places we've dug up and photographed, numbered and analysed; carting away what we could, and exposing what's left to the tourist's glassy gaze.

Perhaps this is why the Yachikel buried him here. Because somewhere in this valley there's a place where the worlds of the living and the dead meet. Where the border between them is thinner than the skin of water, and crossing over is as easy as dipping a hand in a stream.

Penelope is buried in the pretty Cotswold village where she grew up, and where her parents still live. It took me weeks to find it because the funeral was private, they didn't put a notice in *The Times*.

I went there in June. A cold day, you'd never know it was summer. The churchyard was deserted, a chill wind raking the grass, ancient yews sunk in shadow, the squat medieval church forbiddingly locked.

The Dale family headstones were located among the more prosperous graves, near the splendidly carved west porch. Some of them dated back to the seventeenth century, their messages of love and loss dappled with lichen and softened by time.

Her grave was at the end of the row, an outrage of raw wet earth. No headstone. I read somewhere that it's best to wait a few months before erecting a stone, to allow the grave to settle. She was down there in a box, under six feet of mud. Let the grave settle.

This isn't real, I thought as I stood shivering, clutching my bunch of carnations. She isn't down there. She can't be.

As I was laying my bouquet, a hand grabbed my shoulder and nearly yanked me off my feet.

'The *fuck* are you doing?' said her brother. I hardly recognised him. He'd grown cadaverously thin, and his handsome features were distorted with rage. For a moment I was terrified. Had he found out what happened in the car park? Then he was thrusting the carnations at my chest, making me stagger. 'Get out! Take your ghastly flowers with you! She's dead! Leave her alone!'

Shaky with relief, I wiped his spit off my cheek. I didn't try to defend myself. Whatever I said would have made it worse.

'Everything all right, Xander?' called a well-to-do man from the other side of the lych gate. An overweight labrador stood panting at his heels.

'Thanks, Dr Willoughby,' Xander replied without taking his eyes off me. 'I'll take care of this.' 'This', not 'him'. As if I were something to be scraped off his shoe.

The doctor grunted and stood his ground, giving me a hard stare. His tweeds were worn but 'good', and beneath his thinning fair hair his smooth square face had the rubicund assurance of his class. *The Dales have standing in the county*, his stare informed me. *If young Xander needs help, he has only to ask.*

Young Xander didn't need help, I was already beating an ignominious retreat. On the train back to London I berated myself. *Stupid, insensitive. Why do you always go too far?*

For days afterwards I worried that Xander would make trouble about my visit to the grave. Would he set the police on me? Although surely they couldn't arrest me for importuning the dead?

*

A hummingbird zips past my ear, and from beneath my feet comes the stream's subterranean gurgle. A hot afternoon and steamy, white drifts of vapour floating among the trees, preventing me from seeing how far down the valley I've come.

I am ragingly hungry and tormented by mosquitoes; I've long since run out of DEET. I keep swapping my machete from hand to hand. Both are blistered and bleeding.

It comes to me without emotion that I am not going to make it out of this alive. If a snake doesn't get me, starvation will. Or a falling tree or an infection, or any number of lethal jungle creatures.

I stare at my fingers gripping the machete. I picture my dead flesh swelling and blackening, eaten by microbes until only my bones are left; then they too crumble to nothing.

I must have been about seven when I learnt about skeletons. I was aghast. Was there really a bony grimace behind each of the faces around me? Brother, sister, parents, schoolfellows, teachers: for months I couldn't look at anyone without imagining the skull behind the features. I couldn't get over the fact that whether they were smiling, sneering, laughing or scowling, the skull beneath the skin remained unmoved. Without expression. It turned them into aliens. It deepened my sense of being apart. Now, standing in this steamy green gloom, I wonder what will happen to my remains – if they're ever found. I hope I won't be sent back to England. For one thing it would be expensive, and Father isn't made of money, as he's fond of reminding us.

It's odd, but until now I haven't thought of my family.

And yet isn't that what you're supposed to do *in extremis?* Think of your loved ones?

Only they aren't my loved ones, not really, and I'm not theirs. Mother might be upset when she learns that I'm dead, at least for a while. I think she did love me when I was a boy. She was nice about the wasps' nest, and patient when I boycotted Marjorie's pink birthday cake out of solidarity with cochineal insects. She even bought me *British Insects Shown to Children* for my ninth birthday; although she drew the line at letting me keep stick insects in my room, I had to resort to lies. But as for Father, Marjorie and Edwin, they don't even like me. They'll merely be annoyed with me for upsetting Mother.

So yes, I think the family will be content to leave my remains in Mexico. Although I'd rather not be flown to San Cristóbal and stuck in some cemetery among strangers; no, bury me in the rainforest, where I can be part of the jungle. Who knows, I might even come back as a mantis.

But it won't be *me,* there's the rub. The man thinking these thoughts will no longer exist.

I try and fail to imagine my own non-being, as I have failed to do since the idea first occurred to me in my teens.

Unless – unless something *does* remain, after all?

And so, in a few trite steps, we return to Penelope. As we always do. The endless, agonising Möbius strip of self-loathing and remorse.

To my right the undergrowth appears less dense, so I head that way. I've given up on the compass, my only aim is to continue downhill. I am almost asleep on my feet. In a daze I slash foliage, hack, shoulder my way through.

Suddenly I'm bursting out into the open. I'm so startled I nearly fall over.

Above me looms a sheer grey rockface, streaked with black lichen and the silver tracks of snails; above that, a misty blur of trees. At the foot of the rockface, not three yards from where I stand, a small bushy tree is laden with those yellow plum-like fruit – which for once are gloriously within reach, and not a monkey in sight. Behind the tree there's a sort of rocky overhang, and from within it comes a faint gurgle of water.

I feel as if I've stumbled into Paradise. Have I really found the stream? *And* food *and* water *and* shelter for the night?

The overhang is too shallow to call a cave, and its roof is low, I have to crouch to enter. It's cooler inside. Hanging tree roots brush my face like hair. From further within comes a subterranean gurgle: it's emanating from that long dark crack at the back. I'm disappointed that the stream is out of reach, but it's hardly a disaster, my water bottle is still half full.

I would have expected this overhang to be a roost for bats, but I can't smell ammonia or see any droppings, that's another stroke of luck. And it's dry underfoot. With my boot I stir the detritus of dead branches. They'd be perfect for a fire – and wonder of wonders, I disturb no snakes or scorpions or even ants.

To my right, a cave cricket sidles into a crevice on pale, stilt-like legs. On the roof, among the dangling tree roots, I make out the small white egg sacs of cave spiders, like tiny moons. I'm fond of cave spiders. I can live with them.

*

Seated cross-legged at the mouth of the overhang, I munch plums, spitting out seeds, falling into another daze. The sky has cleared and the sun has burnt off the mist. It's only three in the afternoon. For once I haven't left it too late to pitch camp.

At the corner of my eye, something glints. It's so bright. It must be man-made. I lurch to my feet.

There it is again, in the jungle above the rockface. Could it possibly be the rescue party? I fumble for my binoculars and scan the trees.

The specimen bottle catches the sun, twisting and turning in the wind where I hung it last night after freeing the mantis. Beside it, a mere thirty yards above me, towers the ceiba.

It's the same tree, no doubt about that. Beside it stand those hunched, waiting boulders.

I lower the binoculars. I stand swaying, struggling to take it in. My gaze wanders over the yellow plums on the bush before the overhang, and my gear laid neatly within.

Despite all my efforts, a whole day of laborious hacking and slashing has taken me in an enormous loop. Some malign power has played me like a fish on a line – then slowly, inexorably, reeled me in, drawing me back to within spitting distance of that dreadful bloodstained tree. Those haunted rocks.

That grave.

Thirty-Seven

I know that I'm dreaming. I remember falling asleep. I was sitting beneath the overhang in a daze of exhaustion, thinking about lighting a fire before the sun went down. Then I was curling up on my side with my head on my rucksack and drifting off.

This is a dream, and Penelope is here. She is standing at the back, near that shadowy crack, almost but not quite within reach. Her arms hang at her sides, her long dark hair frames her matchless face. Her gaze is accusing. *Why couldn't you leave me alone?*

I try to speak, to tell her that I'm sorry, I should never have written that letter or followed her to the car park – but before I can utter a word, something in my chest splits open and I'm breaking into wrenching sobs. Abject in the dust, I gasp out my longing and despair. Her face never changes. *Why couldn't you leave me alone?*

I'm still crying when I wake up. My eyes are swollen and sore, my cheeks wet with tears.

It's dark. I've no idea of the time, my watch has stopped at ten past four. As in the dream, I am lying curled on my side with my head on the rucksack, beside the unlit makings of the fire. Beneath me, through the earth, I catch the subterranean gurgle of water.

Sitting up, I grope in the rucksack for my torch. I clutch it but don't switch it on. Under the gurgle of water I catch a distant murmur of wind: an echoing, wordless, ever-changing voice.

In the world outside, a faint breeze stirs the plum tree, and in its shadowy foliage, tiny pale-green sparks are blinking on and off. Fireflies. Numbly I sit and watch them.

That's when I sense her behind me. As in the dream, she is standing at the back of the overhang, near the crack. Almost but not quite within reach.

As in the dream, her face is bitter. Accusing. Her lips move, but no sound comes.

Silently berating me, she turns and disappears into the dark.

With a moan I crawl after her. I snap on my torch. Rocks lurch, tree roots leap from the shadows, brushing my face like hair. The roots of the ceiba are warning me back.

The crack is a mouth of absolute blackness. Penelope is down there. On hands and knees I shuffle closer.

The crack is wider than I thought: wide enough to take me, if I edge in sideways. I shine my torch into it, the feeble yellow beam revealing a steep descent. From within comes a cold, earthy exhalation and a distant murmur of wind and water: rising and falling, now louder, now dying to nothing.

Xibalba. The place where Kayun heard the screams of the wind being born.

Part of me shrinks from it in horror. If I go down there

I will never come out. And yet a deeper part of me isn't even surprised.

Everything I've done since Penelope was killed has brought me to this place. This is why I left England and travelled to Mexico. This is why I came to the jungle. She is down there. Waiting for me.

It flashes across my mind that it isn't really her. It's Ka-yun's brother, the shape-shifting *akij* who can take any form. But I have to take that chance. I cannot *not* follow her.

Over my shoulder I take a last look at the world above: at the fireflies glimmering among the plum tree's black leaves.

Then I turn my back on the world and follow her in.

Thirty-Eight

The Maya believed that if you go underground, you die. Is that what I'm doing? Looking for death?

My breath is alarmingly loud in this cramped space. My torch beam reveals folds of reddish stone like dank cold flesh. The crack is so narrow that to get through it I have to stretch one arm forwards and one arm back; so low that I can't lift my head. Lying on my stomach, I squirm like a snake, pushing forwards with my toes. I am coffined in unyielding rock. Oh God oh God what if I'm stuck? Trapped under millions of tons of rock. How long will I take to die?

Steady. Don't breathe so deeply, you're making it worse. Shallow and slow. That's it.

The tunnel drops steeply into impenetrable dark. Penelope is down there. I have to find her.

The beam flickers. Battery's almost dead. I ought to save it for when I need it most. I switch it off, and darkness presses on my eyeballs. Like a blind man I feel my way, my torch clinking against stone. The voices of wind and water have died to nothing. All I can hear is clink, clink. My gasping breath.

Suddenly my torch strikes empty air. I toe myself

forwards, I sense space opening around me, blessed, blessed space. Cautiously I pass the torch above my head. More empty air.

Shuddering with relief, I haul myself to all fours. I sit back on my heels – and nearly fall over. The darkness is absolute, I can't tell up from down.

Silence beats at my ears: the unending silence of inanimate stone. The stillness, the unbearable stillness. I have left the world of the living. This is what it's like to be dead.

Putting my palm to my face, I feel my nose, my damp breath warming my skin – but I can't see my hand. I turn my head, straining to see something, anything. If I can neither hear nor see, how do I know I exist? Perhaps I'm already dead. Already part of this unending silence.

'Penelope,' I whisper. My voice sounds harsh. Frightened.

She isn't here. I can feel it. Why has she led me underground, only to abandon me? What does she want?

Or wasn't it her?

I can't face what that might mean. I grind my knuckles into my eyes, creating faint webs of light that come and go, like the afterglow of fireflies. I switch on the torch. The glare is blinding, I shield it with my free hand. But the light steadies me.

Dimly above my head I catch the pallid glimmer of stalactites. Around me rise stalagmites, grey figures shrouded in glistening stone. Clutching my torch, I crawl forwards. Shadows leap. Faces come at me from the gloom: gaping mouths and blind black eyes. I know they are my brain's attempt to people the inanimate dark, but I'm still afraid. I can feel their intent.

My shadow is enormous and misshapen. One moment it's behind me, the next it's arching overhead. It doesn't belong to me any more, I dare not look in case I catch it moving by itself. I have become scared of my own shadow.

There is something at the back of the cave. My beam can't reach it, I perceive it only by contrast: black upon black. Part of the roof has fallen in, piling earth onto a tilted slab of stone.

I'm not sure why, but that earthen mound feels wrong. And yet I'm crawling closer.

I kneel on something which snaps beneath me. It's a clay bowl. Here's another. My torch reveals pottery everywhere, piled on the floor, tucked into niches and between stalagmites: beakers, dishes, jars lidded with monstrous snarling faces. Some are glazed black or rusty red, many painted in that free-flowing style I know from the dig. In my faltering beam, disjointed images leap from the dark: a fist grasping a snake, a cluster of impossibly complex Mayan glyphs. The grinning skull and bloated belly of the rotting god of death.

Sensing something more, I raise my torch.

To my left, in a niche above my head, stands a pillar the colour of the moon. Its ancient carvings are impenetrably dense, but at their centre I make out the figure of a man in a plumed headdress. Impassive, he stares out of the past. He is seated with splayed legs, and in one hand he grasps a leaf-shaped blade. I dip my torch, shrouding him in darkness.

At the foot of the pillar lies a shrivelled scrap of spotted fur and several long feathers of faded greenish-blue.

Beside them, a bunch of red plastic tulips and a Yachikel gourd full of blue glass marbles. Kayun has been here before me. Before him, his nameless, faceless brother – and before him many others, stretching all the way back. All have left offerings. I must do the same. Perhaps this is why she led me here. She wants me to relinquish my last link to her. Perhaps then she will be appeased.

Unzipping my breast pocket, I take out the talisman.

My throat closes, my eyes burn. For the final time I unwrap the handkerchief and touch her hair. Then I snap the twig in two and place it at the foot of the pillar.

'There,' I say harshly. 'That's the last link cut.'

It isn't enough. I know that as clearly as if it's been spoken out loud. What haunts this place wants more.

I notice a shard of black obsidian lying beside the gourd. Leaf-shaped, the length of my middle finger. The moment I pick it up, an image flashes at me: a black edge slicing, flesh parting like wet red lips, blood bubbling. Cut, cut.

My heart is knocking against my ribs. I was wrong to come here. I am a hunted creature, I have to get away. But instead of turning round, I am crawling past the pillar towards the back of the cave, clutching the obsidian blade in my free hand. That lopsided thing on its tilted stone is waiting for me. I can't bear to go nearer, and yet I must.

As I crawl, my torch reveals giant red glyphs boldly daubed on the pale stone walls. I don't know what they mean, I don't want to know, but I recognise one: a hand grasping a spike. *Tzak*. To conjure by shedding blood.

And there's another, a hand with droplets raining from between forefinger and thumb. *Chok*. Scatter.

In my mind I see the picture in the book on the plane. The priest thrusting a blade through his penis. Scarlet snakes spurting in bloody orgasm.

My heart is hammering. No no, that can't be what it wants.

Some of the glyphs are smeared with rusty brown. I lean closer. I catch a metallic whiff of blood. Cut, cut.

Panting, I crawl towards the dark at the back of the cave.

A distant echo of water breaks the silence: then a murmur of wind. With jarring suddenness I crawl into icy cold, the change as shocking as if I've opened a door on winter. In the failing light my breath smokes. My skin is prickling. The frosty air crackles with menace.

Dimly, I make out the lopsided mound of earth. It moves, though my torch does not.

I stop breathing. That is no pile of earth. It's a bundle. Squat, man-sized, swathed in many layers of stained cloth. They didn't bury him at the tree. They brought him here.

I can't bear to look at the bundled corpse, and yet I can't avert my eyes. The voices of wind and water are rising, a wordless clamour beating in my skull.

A corner of the outer layer lifts, wavers, gropes blindly at air. Slowly it begins to unpeel.

Another layer lifts and peels back. Then another. Jerkily, inexorably, layer upon layer. Unwrapping itself.

Cut. Cut.

No! I scream inside my head.

Now only the final layer remains, clinging to the bony figure that crouches within. Now that layer too is peeling away. I make out a torrent of brittle black hair. Mottled skin stretched over a ridged spine, shoulder blades sharp as knives. If it turns to face me, my heart will burst.

I am still clutching the obsidian blade. Cut. Cut.

My torch blinks out.

Green daylight in the jungle. A tattooed brown fist raises a knife and slashes a brown throat. The hot arterial spray splashes bark and rock.

With my free hand I feel for my throat, my carotid pulse. I see my life spattering the glyphs on the moon-coloured stone. This is what it wants. Always this.

I try to shout that I'm sorry, but what comes out is a voiceless wheeze. Clutching the blade, I bring it to my throat. Cut, cut.

In the last instant I drop my hand to my waist and fumble for my crotch. I grab flesh and cut.

Animal screams filling the cave, bouncing off rock, battering my brain. Still screaming, I smear the glyphs with my blood. I crawl back through the cave, not daring to glance behind me in case it's following.

Still screaming, I claw my way up the tunnel. I burst out, I stagger from the overhang into a raging chaos of wind and rain.

A dazzle of green lightning, a deafening crack of thunder. Then a great rending groan – and as I raise my head I see the ceiba crashing towards me.

The last thing I know before I collapse is wet leaf mould pressing my face and hot blood flooding my thighs.

Thirty-Nine

I am lying on my side in the topmost branches of the ceiba. Around me twigs sprout and leaves unfurl. A flower opens to the sky, which is slowly growing light.

Drowsily I watch the flower's waxy petals curling back. My eye takes in its russet core and its thick white clustered stamens, each tipped with ochrous red. I am warm and completely at peace. Goodbye, Penelope. Goodbye, life.

Before my face I make out my blood-stained fist, clenching something which used to matter. Beside it is a leaf, and on the leaf is a mantis. My gaze wanders lovingly over her gorgeous alien head. The lethal perfection of her forelegs, the blue-green iridescence of her folded wings.

Curiosity flickers: among mantids, iridescence is rarest of the rare. What species are you, beautiful one? What do you see when you look at me? Have you come to help me die?

I'm too peaceful to hold onto the thoughts. Closing my eyes, I drift away.

Now colours are turning in my head: radiant sapphire, a sunburst of gold, the vital crimson of a beating heart.

Entranced, I watch the colours spiral together – resolve into feathers – and become a scarlet macaw.

The great bird perches on the tree at the centre of the world. It peers down at me and I meet its ageless eye. Now it is spreading its glorious wings and taking flight – and I am flying too. I *am* the macaw. I am gazing down at the moon and the last pale stars, at the ceaseless stirring of the emerald forest.

For one miraculous instant I see *everything*. I see raindrops trembling on every filament of every spider's web; the translucent pulse in the throat of every frog. I see through the bark of every tree to its coursing sap, through the flesh of every creature to its jostling corpuscles. For this one instant of piercing joy I am part of it all. I am a singing thread of light.

Then with a jolt I am down on the ground, lying on my side, rain pattering on my face, watching a mantis on a leaf watching me.

That was how they found me. Lying on my side in a patch of wet leaf mould, half-covered by the fallen ceiba's topmost branches.

It was my light-coloured clothes which saved me. J.C. noticed the red stain at my crotch and staunched the bleeding with spiders' webs and moss.

I found out later that he was the one who'd raised the alarm; but only after he'd lost his way after leaving me, and had spent a night alone in the jungle.

Or that's what he said happened. I've never asked him if he abandoned me on purpose. Even if he did, he thought better of it. Weeks later, Ridley told me that the boy was frantic when he arrived in camp, and indefatigable in the search party. It was thanks to his tracking skills that they found me at all.

Ridley was also part of the rescue party, as were Marshall, Watts, one of the guards, and Dr Mendoza; Birkenshaw had remained in camp to keep an eye on things.

To my surprise, the Professor came too. He stayed with me while Dr Mendoza turned me onto my back and propped my feet on a log and dressed my wound. I was in shock and feeling no pain, but intensely cold; the Professor wrapped me in a blanket.

At one point he asked if I had any gear which he could send the men to fetch. I was about to tell him that my rucksack was in the overhang, but I changed my mind. 'I lost it,' I lied.

J.C., squatting nearby, briefly met my eyes, and I realised that he knew about the overhang, and the cave to which it leads. That cave which now lies hidden beneath the fallen ceiba, concealed from Westerners – although not from the Yachikel.

Poor Professor Atkinson. He will never learn how close he came to making the find of a lifetime. That cave would have made his name – and mine too. An underground shrine of the ancient Maya, lost for centuries. The stuff of dreams.

But lost to whom? Not to the Yachikel. They've always known of it. All they want is for us to leave it alone.

Well, they've got their wish. No one will find it now.

As a scientist, I'm aware that the ceiba fell because it was struck by lightning. I also know that Kayun believes that it fell to protect the cave, and that it was brought down by his brother, who by his death became one with the gods. Perhaps he also thinks that my offering of blood played its part too.

I don't pity the Professor, he can do without the cave. Besides, he has his ways of funding the dig. And realising what they are has enabled me to make my own accommodation with him.

On the way back to camp, Dr Mendoza asked me how I sustained my injury, and I told him it was when the ceiba nearly crushed me; but he's no fool, he knows the difference between a wound caused by a branch, and an obsidian blade.

He must have voiced his suspicions to the Professor, who came to see me a few days later in the hospital in San Cristóbal.

'Tell me why you hurt yourself,' he said without preamble, smoking one of his cigars in casual defiance of the nurses.

'I didn't,' I said without opening my eyes. 'It was the ceiba. If it had fallen a foot closer I'd have been squashed like an ant.'

'Come now, Corbett. Mendoza's sure you did it yourself.'

I opened my eyes and looked at him.

He leaned closer. 'You do know that I'll have to inform the Institute?'

He didn't need to spell out the rest. If he reported half what I'd done – my illicit forays upriver, getting lost, the self-mutilation – I could kiss goodbye to tenure, not to mention my career.

That's when I decided to make use of what I'd surmised about his own little matter during my enforced idleness in hospital. 'That VIP from the Foundation,' I said quietly. 'Dr Herrera.'

The rugged face went still.

'He didn't come to discuss funding the dig,' I went on. 'At least, not directly.'

He was watching me intently.

'Ridley,' I said, 'fixes more than relations with the Indians. He introduced you to Dr Herrera. Who deals in pre-Columbian art.'

A long silence. The Professor studied his cigar. Tapped it against the edge of the bedside cabinet. Frowned at the ash on the floor, scuffed it under the bed with his boot. 'It was only the one time,' he said. 'Couple of ceramic incense burners. Commonplace. Not remotely significant.'

I didn't believe him. From what I'd seen, he and Dr Herrera were too at ease with each other to have met for the first time this season.

The Professor drew a breath. 'I did it to fund the dig, you understand. I kept nothing for myself.'

I wasn't sure if I believed that either, but I told him that I did. I felt sorry for him: a dreamer compromised by his own ambition. That's why he tolerates Ridley and Birkenshaw's predilections, and Mendoza's drinking. They all know – or at least they suspect about the thefts.

I watched him sit straighter and square his shoulders. He thrust out his chin: the hero facing the firing squad. 'What will you do?' he said.

I let him sweat for a bit. I felt he owed me that after his bombast at our first meeting. 'Nothing,' I said at last.

'That is, if... You see, Professor. I shall want to come back here. Continue my work.'

He blinked. 'After what you've been through?'

'Yes.'

He considered that. Then slowly nodded. 'I can arrange that. Square things with the Institute.'

I smiled. 'Good. Then we'll say no more about it.'

There was someone else in the rescue party. Kayun.

I didn't fool myself that he'd come out of concern for me. He came to make sure that no one found the cave. That cave has been sacred since the time of his ancestors. His brother died for it. Kayun means to keep it safe.

I think now that he wanted me to find it all along. He wanted my blood to help protect it. Why me? Perhaps to punish me for fogging his sacred trees. Or perhaps it didn't matter who it was, he simply needed to punish a *ts'ul* for the sufferings of his people.

He's already taken his revenge on the Professor. That's why Ridley pays him, to keep quiet about the thefts. And perhaps Kayun's revenge has a more personal element too, the satisfaction of knowing that by keeping the cave secret, he is depriving the Professor of the find that would make his career.

What does Kayun think of me now? I've often wondered. At one point soon after they found me I was briefly alone with him, so I seized my chance: I opened my fist and showed him what I'd been clutching all that time. Without a word he took the obsidian blade, wiped it clean of my blood with a clump of moss, and stowed it in the pouch at his belt.

'I won't ever tell,' I murmured.

He heard me, though he didn't reply. He didn't even look at me. He simply got up and walked away.

But I didn't expect to be thanked. I'd had my reward. What haunts that place let me live.

People think it's odd that I keep returning to the jungle which nearly killed me, but the truth is I can't stay away. It's where I feel most alive.

It's easier now that I've got tenure. That fell into place shortly after I recovered. I'd stayed on thanks to the Professor, and in the weeks that remained, I found a species of mantid new to science.

Since then I've been back many times. Naturally I no longer fog ceibas, I find my mantids by other means, often purely by looking; although I've never found that iridescent one who was with me when I was dying. Perhaps she was part of my vision – like the ceiba's waxy flowers, which I couldn't have seen because it wasn't the right season – but I don't think so. The veining on her wings was too specific, and the shape of her mesothorax. I like to think that she was a sign from the jungle that I've been forgiven for fogging those ceibas. Which is illogical, but I don't care. Every time I think of her, my spirit lifts.

So I go on searching. To date I've published two papers on novel behaviours of arboreal mantids, and found two more species new to science. I make that distinction because J.C. says they've been known to the Yachikel for centuries. J.C. has helped me a good deal in my work. I'm no closer to understanding him, or what he hopes to achieve in life; but we get along well, and I like to think we've become friends.

He continues quietly to evade Ridley's advances. Just as success continues to evade the Professor, and self-respect will always be beyond Birkenshaw's reach. So in some ways, I've been luckier than most.

I'm well aware that in the scheme of things, my work doesn't amount to much. But I tell myself that if I can reveal something of value to science, and pass on a trace of what I feel for my mantids – their grace, their beauty, their mystery – I might help save them, and the jungle in which they live.

Though I've no illusions. If the Professor is right, and the ancient Maya collapsed because they took too much from the forest, they only did what we're doing now. Even the Yachikel are selling their great trees. Taking too much is what people have been doing since we first began walking on two legs.

It still hurts when I think of Penelope, but not as savagely as before. That part of myself I cut away and left in the cave, and I've been better without it. I hated being in love. Now I'm free.

I will never know if what I did played a part in her death, and that's my punishment. Poor little Penelope. It wasn't her fault that I became obsessed. I was like a moth circling a nightlight, I mistook her for the moon. Even after she died, I went on trying to reach her. Her brother was right: *Leave her alone. Stop stalking a ghost.*

With the Professor's permission I work mainly upriver in the old-growth forest, although I don't venture in far, and

I haven't tried to find that valley where the monkeys have never seen man. Or the cave.

But I think of it every day. Because there's another reason I keep returning to the jungle, and it has nothing to do with mantids. It's the memory of that moment when I was dying. When I flew up from the tree of life and became a singing thread of light.

That's really what brings me back year after year. The hope that one day, at some future time, I will become that again.

Author's Note

I first experienced the rainforest in the late 1990s, when I travelled by motorised dugout up a tributary of the Peruvian Amazon. I stayed at a rudimentary eco-lodge, and spent days happily exploring the rainforest. Then in 2018 I visited the rainforests of Costa Rica and was entranced all over again.

For years I'd had a vague idea of setting a ghost story in a jungle, so on both trips I'd taken extensive notes. But nothing had come of it, and by 2021 I was struggling with the pandemic, family demands and a nasty stretch of writer's block. I'd never experienced it before and it lasted most of the year. Then two weeks before Christmas the drought finally broke, and the idea for *Rainforest* arrived like a tropical downpour.

I made up the principal places in the story, namely the Yachikel village and the ruins of Piedras Quemadas. Both are located on an invented tributary of the real Rio Lacantún, itself a tributary of the Rio Usumacinta, which forms the border between Mexico and Guatemala.

However, much of what Simon encounters is based on my own experiences in rainforests. In Peru I ate manioc (cassava) and fried piranha; I encountered tarantulas, millipedes, capybara, caiman and bullet ants, among other creatures. I hiked through tropical downpours, including a memorably violent storm; afterwards, like Simon, my scalp was gritty with debris washed down from the canopy.

Costa Rica introduced me to the basilisk lizard, howler monkeys, snakebirds, toucans, drunken butterflies and morphos; plus several breathtaking encounters with macaws, the dead bird which Simon finds on the fifth terrace (a manakin), and lots more besides. I came across ceiba trees in Jamaica, Peru and Costa Rica. I've always been struck by their formidable presence, and by the rich and often fearful folklore they inspire.

I also made up the Yachikel people, drawing on the beliefs and ways of life of modern Maya, particularly the Lacandon, Quiché, Yucatec and Zinecantecos. For the Yachikel language I've borrowed or adapted words from Lacandon and other Mayan languages, including Quiché, Yucatec and Kaqchikel. I didn't invent the Yachikel's polygamy, underage wives, sexual segregation and inbreeding: all are seen in certain indigenous rainforest peoples. Some of my Indian guides in the Peruvian Amazon helped provide inspiration for J.C.

Kayun's shamanism is based on the beliefs of some modern Maya, as well as those of other peoples, such as the Huichol (Wixárika) and Yanomami. I made up *muktan*, although its effects have elements in common with several plant alkaloids, including mescaline, peyote and ayahuasca. As an aside, the Lacandon used to regard mantids as special; perhaps they still do.

One important point: I hope readers appreciate that in the story, the derogatory attitudes of many of the Westerners to the Yachikel are no reflection of my own views. I've simply tried to show how indigenous people tended to be perceived in the early 1970s, when the story is set.

Concerning the ancient Maya, the fictional Piedras Quemadas is principally based on the real sites at Tonina, Yaxchilan and Palenque. The carvings and artefacts which Simon comes across derive from real ones from the Classic period. And I've tried to make what Birkenshaw and his colleagues know about the ancient Maya reflect the state of archaeological knowledge in 1973. The only exception of which I'm aware is that in the 1970s the meaning of certain Mayan glyphs had yet to be deciphered; but if I've jumped the gun by a few years in this respect, I think that's acceptable in a work of fiction.

A quick word on usage, namely whether one should say 'Mayan' or 'Maya' when referring to something pertaining to their culture. Mayanists tend to refer to the 'Mayan' language, and to everything else – be it history, art, religion or whatever – as 'Maya'. But having said that, the eminent translator of my edition of the *Popol Vuh*, the great Maya Book of Creation, uses the term 'Mayan' more broadly in his Introduction. So in the story I haven't been a stickler on this, and neither is Simon. We are, after all, both laymen.

I also want to say a word about the bloodthirsty nature of the ancient Maya. Lest anyone thinks I've sensationalised them, I didn't make up any of their customs or beliefs as featured in the story. Decapitation, torture and self-mutilation are prominent in the art and writings of the ancient Maya. The graphic depiction of penile blood-letting which nauseates Simon is based on real ones, particularly those at San Bartolo; while the blood serpents appear in many depictions of blood-letting and sacrifice, such as those at Chichen Itza. The frescoes Simon mentions are those at Bonampak – which, when two Americans discovered them in 1946, overturned western perceptions of the ancient Maya. The only thing I'm aware of inventing is Ridley's idea that the ancient Maya resorted to suicide as a shortcut to heaven; and that, as Birkenshaw points out, is a layman's speculation.

Concerning Simon's beloved mantids, I first fell under their spell – and not in a good way – when I was eleven years old, staying with my grandparents in what was then Natal, South Africa. My nightly trips to the loo were made purgatorial by mantids of all shapes and sizes which lurked on the bathroom walls, attracted by the light which my well-meaning parents had left on, to reassure me and my sister. It was years before I came to admire mantids; and then not quite as fervently as does Simon.

What he knows about them broadly reflects the state of knowledge in the 1970s. This includes his belief that mantids can't hear. Scientists only discovered in the 1980s that many mantids do have a form of ear, located in the thorax.

For the interested reader, here are the principal books I found useful. On the ancient Maya: *The Maya* (M. Coe, Thames and Hudson, 1984); *Maya Art and Architecture* (M. E. Miller, Thames and Hudson, 1999); *The South American*

Handbook 1973 (Trade & Travel Publications Ltd); *The Gods and Symbols of Ancient Mexico and the Maya* (M. E. Miller & K. Taube, Thames and Hudson, 1993); *Popol Vuh* (transl. D. Tedlock, Simon & Schuster, 1996); *Handbook to Life in the Ancient Maya World* (L .V. Foster, Facts on File, Inc, 2002).

On modern Maya, indigenous rainforest people and shamanism: *The Last Lords of Palenque* (V. Perera & R. D. Bruce, University of California Press, 1982); *The Zinecantecos of Mexico* (E. Z. Vogt, Holt, Rinehart & Winston, 1970); *Jungle Quest* (H. Rittlinger, Odhams Press, 1959); *Secret of the Forest* (W. Cordan, Gollancz, 1963); *Shamanism* (M. Eliade, Princeton University Press, 1964); *Shamanic Voices* (J. Halifax, E. P. Dutton, 1979).

On mantids, rainforest wildlife and ecology: *Grasshoppers & Mantids of the World* (K. Preston-Mafham, Cassell Plc, 1992); *The Praying Mantids* (ed. F. R. Prete et al., The Johns Hopkins University Press, 1999); *Insects and other Arthropods of Tropical America* (P. E. Hanson & K. Nishida, Cornell University Press, 2016); *Travellers' Wildlife Guide to Belize & Northern Guatemala* (L. Beletsky, Arris Publishing Ltd, 2005); *A Field Guide to the Amphibians and Reptiles of the Maya World* (J C. Lee, Cornell University Press, 2000).

On Westerners' experiences of the rainforest, including being lost: *Ruthless River* (H. Fitzgerald, Penguin, 2017); *Lost in the Jungle* (Y. Ghinsberg, Summersdale Publishers Ltd, 2008); *Keep the River on Your Right* (T. Schneebaum, GMP Publishers Ltd, 1988); *Mother of God* (P. Rosolie, HarperCollins, 2014); *Walking the Jungle* (J. Coningham, Burford Books, 2003).

Of course, any mistakes in the story are down to me.

Finally, I need to thank some people. My thanks to the numerous guides on my rainforest trips who helped me experience the jungle and its inhabitants. I am enormously grateful to my analyst Julia Ovchinnikova, as it's thanks to her that I was able to break through my writer's block and come up with the idea for *Rainforest*. Huge thanks to my editor Samantha Eades at Orion Books, who grasped at once what I was trying to achieve, and whose searching comments helped me make it a better book; and to Leodora Darlington, who took over with such energy and enthusiasm when Sam left. Finally, much gratitude as always to my agent Peter Cox of Redhammer Limited: for giving me the time and space to get through the writer's block; his willingness to be told nothing about the story while I was writing it; and his enthusiastic support when I finally let him see the completed typescript.

Michelle Paver
London, 2025